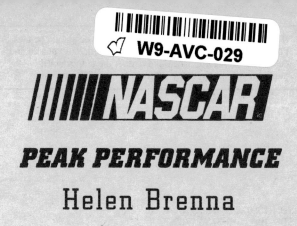

NASCAR

PEAK PERFORMANCE

Helen Brenna

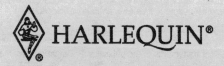

HARLEQUIN®

TORONTO • NEW YORK • LONDON
AMSTERDAM • PARIS • SYDNEY • HAMBURG
STOCKHOLM • ATHENS • TOKYO • MILAN • MADRID
PRAGUE • WARSAW • BUDAPEST • AUCKLAND

ISBN-13: 978-0-373-21789-2
ISBN-10:   0-373-21789-7

PEAK PERFORMANCE

HELEN BRENNA

grew up the seventh of eight children in central Minnesota. Although as a child she never dreamed of writing novels, she must have assimilated the necessary skills from her storytelling brothers.

She earned a degree in accounting and worked for years as a CPA, but the decision to stay home with her kids changed everything. After winning the prestigious Maggie Award for romance writers, her new career took off and she hasn't yet looked back.

Helen still lives in Minnesota with her husband, two children, two dogs and three cats and would love hearing from you. E-mail her at helenbrenna@comcast.net, or send mail to P.O. Box 24107, Minneapolis, MN 55424.

Visit her Web site at helenbrenna.com or chat with Helen and several other writers at ridingwiththetopdown.blogspot.com.

For Dylan,
my sunshine

ACKNOWLEDGMENTS

Special thanks to Jason Wiltse who put himself out there, spending hours touring me around his TV station, introducing me to people, answering my rudimentary questions and being an all-around great guy. And thanks to Steve Johnson for his invaluable insight into the world of sports broadcasting.

I'd also like to thank Scott Backes, my first belay! Years and years ago he helped me feel safe at the end of a rope. Though I never climbed anything close to El Cap, I did get a few calluses and spectacular bruises for my amateurish efforts.

Thanks, my precious Princesses, for your patience and support.

You, too, Tina Wexler. Marsha Zinberg and Tina Colombo, thanks for this opportunity.

And finally Mary and Dennis Kuryla…
you know this is all your fault!

NASCAR spotter Steve Grosso wanted nothing more than to convince his girlfriend, veterinarian Heidi Kramer, to marry him...even though Heidi balked at living on the NASCAR circuit. Both Steve and Heidi realized that in order to make their relationship work, they had to try some seriously risky moves!

CHAPTER ONE

"LIKE A SNAPPY LUBE on steroids," Payton Reese grumbled to himself. Team members hustled this way and that, the buzz of engines getting last-minute adjustments bounced off the trailers and the pungent smell of oil and gasoline filled the early-evening Virginia air. "What did I get myself into?"

"Whaddya say?" His cameraman, Neil Bukowski, flipped his baseball cap backward and got ready to tape.

Payton refocused, reminding himself this duty was temporary. This job and these interviews were a means to an end. Six more months max and all the noise, the crowds and smelly stock-car fumes would be nothing but a bad memory.

"I said where the hell is Rachel Murphy?"

NASCAR had arranged for him and his television station, WJAZ 11, to have unlimited access to the entire Murphy family for the weekend. Since qualifying runs, which determined starting positions for tonight's race, he'd had plenty of time with Justin Murphy, Justin's uncle Hugo and the Fulcrum Racing team, but not one second with Justin's sister, Rachel.

"Might be a long shot," Neil said, his southern twang edged with sarcasm. "But I'm gonna guess that an engine specialist spends a bit of time in the garage."

His co-workers had been giving Payton crap since the day he started on the job several months back. In the beginning, most of their comments had been downright nasty, but then Payton had hung some pictures on his office walls of Denali, K2, Cerro Torre and other mountains he'd climbed through the years, and suddenly all that ribbing had turned decidedly good-natured.

They had a point, though. Charlotte's newest sportscaster *should* know a thing or two about NASCAR. Then again, how complicated could this sport be? Popular as all get-out, but it wasn't rocket science.

"Yeah, but which one is the Fulcrum garage?" he asked.

"Over there." Neil balanced his camera on his shoulder with his right arm and pointed with his left. "See the one with the No. 448 car in it?"

Justin Murphy's car. *Duh.* Payton passed several garage stalls at the Richmond track and ignored the throbbing in his back. He'd have to get some heat on it pretty soon to make it through the race.

Keep moving. Just keep moving.

Justin's carefree laugh sounded above the rest of the ruckus before Payton spotted his dark brown head bent in conversation with his uncle Hugo, Fulcrum's crew chief; his second cousin and spotter, Dennis Murphy; and another man Payton had yet to meet. He signaled to Neil. "Start taping."

"Now?"

"You never know what clip's gonna come in handy." He smiled. "Hey, Justin."

The driver glanced up, and his expression turned cautious, as if bracing himself for an onslaught from some crazed fan. Payton couldn't blame the guy, especially not after watching him at the hospitality tent. Everyone had wanted a piece of him, from teenagers to grandmothers, toddlers to grown men.

Once he recognized Payton, he visibly relaxed. "Well, if it isn't Mister J-A-Z."

Payton nodded at Justin's uncle and cousin. "Hugo. Dennis."

"Payton, have you met Wade Abraham?" Hugo patted the back of the man sitting next to him. "He's our car chief."

Hair, skin and eyes all dark, the man looked more model than mechanic to Payton.

"Wade, this is Payton Reese, WJAZ's sportscaster for a brand-new show they're calling *On the Road.*"

"Hey, Payton."

Payton shook the man's hand and immediately noticed the strong muscles in his forearms. *Coulda been a climber.* "How do you like working for Fulcrum, Wade?"

"Dream come true, that's for sure." Wade grinned. "I'm learning a lot working for Hugo."

Payton studied the darkening sky. "Think the rain'll hold off until after the race?"

"Not a chance," Dennis said.

"I don't know about that," Hugo said. "Last time I checked, the radar was looking pretty good." He tipped his head toward Neil. "You still taping?"

"Yes, sir, if it's all right," Payton said. "We'll wrap things up tonight after the race is over. That is, *if* I can get some time to talk with Rachel."

The Fulcrum men glanced at each other and snickered.

"She still avoidin' you?" Hugo asked.

"Sure seems like it." The most he'd ever seen of Rachel was the back of her orange-and-brown Turn-Rite

Tools uniform. He and Neil would walk into a room, and she'd walk out.

Normally, he wouldn't think twice about a woman avoiding him. Some had better common sense than others. Problem was he'd assured his new boss the first episode of *On the Road*'s NASCAR Families series would be completed by the end of this week, and a special about the Murphys wouldn't be complete without Rachel, daughter of the late Troy Murphy and one of the few women fundamentally involved in racing operations these days.

His boss's warning came back to taunt Payton. *You do a special on the Murphys first, you might not get the Grossos. Do the Grossos first, and you might not get the Murphys. Either way, you'll never get Rachel.*

"She's in there." Hugo signaled toward the interior of the garage. "Going through her lists for the tenth time. Head on in there. She won't bite."

"Much," Justin added with a grin.

Bite all you want, sweetheart. With any luck, it'd take his mind off the pain in his back.

Payton headed into the garage with Neil following him. It was cooler in the shade, especially with the concrete floor. Rows of fluorescent lights hung overhead, and several guys in Turn-Rite getups leaning against a tool cabinet acknowledged him as he walked by.

As he rounded the back of Justin's car, he spotted, poking out from under the hood, the cutest female bottom he'd ever seen. Stopping for a second, he admired her lines. Yep, he'd bivy up with Rachel Murphy any old time.

Behind him, Neil cleared his throat.

Payton took another step and entered her peripheral line of vision. "Rachel?"

"What?" She hadn't exactly snapped at him, but she hadn't warmly welcomed him, either. Her long, reddish ponytail stuck out from the back of the Fulcrum Racing baseball cap. He'd been surprised to find she had long, wavy hair. He'd pictured a woman engine specialist with a short, no-nonsense cut.

When she didn't come out from under the hood, he moved to her other side for a better glimpse of her profile. She might have grease smudged on her cheek and neck, but there was nothing masculine about this woman. Matter of fact, she was kind of cute.

Strangely enough, cute made him nervous. "What's a pretty lady like you doing in a greasy pit like this?" *Did he really say that?*

She turned her head slightly and, even in the shadow of the hood, he saw her hazel eyes flashing, felt the burn of a nasty comeback forming in her mouth. He braced himself for the icebreaker, got ready to chuckle it off for being such a fool, but nothing came. She went back to her engine.

"Yeah, I know." He decided to help her out. "Just what you need. A funny guy." Now he'd pissed her off. He laughed anyway, thrown off his mark. "I'm Payton Reese. Sportscaster with WJA—"

"I know who you are."

"We're doing a special on your family."

"Good for you." She came out from under the hood balancing several spark plugs in one hand while examining another one with a magnifying glass.

The engine she was working on looked like nothing he'd ever seen before. "Want some help with that?"

Her eyebrows formed an are-you-out-of-your-mind arch.

"Good call. I don't know diddly about cars." He flashed

her a grin. When in doubt, it usually worked with women. Not this one. Common sense in spades. Completely unfazed, she tossed a spark plug into the garbage, grabbed another one, studied it and submerged herself under the hood again.

So much for small talk. "Not many women involved in NASCAR operations. How'd you get to be an engine specialist?"

She didn't bother answering that one.

"A Murphy. Right. I'm full of dumb questions." This was going nowhere. He caught Neil's eye and dragged his finger across his throat. With only a shrug as final encouragement, the lanky guy turned around and loped away. "I called off the cameraman, okay, Rachel?" Payton said. "Can we chat for a few minutes?"

She glanced back at him, suspicion lingering. After ducking out from under the hood, she wiped her hands on a clean rag and watched Neil head out of the garage. A petite thing, she was a good head shorter than him.

"The race is starting soon," she said.

He could definitely take that as a no. "Can I find you after the race?"

"You can try."

"All right then, I'll *try* to catch you later." He tipped his hand and stayed positive. "Good luck tonight. Hope the weather holds."

By the time he joined back up with Neil, Hugo and Justin were long gone. Frustrated, Payton headed away from the Fulcrum garage, not sure where he was heading. He turned to Neil. "Man alive, is she cagey."

"Can you blame her?"

"What am I missing?"

"I'm surprised you didn't find it in your research."

"Read a lot about the Murphys." There wasn't much specifically about Rachel, except for tidbits like graduating summa cumm laude from Virginia Tech. She was one smart cookie. "What happened?"

"Several years ago some reporter got out of hand. Asked how much truth there was to the rumor that her dad's screwing around had caused her mother's suicide."

Payton cringed. No wonder. His research had indicated Rachel had only been about two when her mother had killed herself. Not long after, her dad had died in a hit-and-run. "Some idiot actually asked that?"

Neil nodded.

"What did Rachel say?"

"Nothin'. Locked right up. Live. On national TV. Hasn't talked to another reporter since."

All the more reason for a decent interview with Rachel. He'd promised his producer something different, something special, something that'd boost the station's ratings, and quiet time with the elusive Rachel Murphy might be his ticket to hosting an extreme sports show at National Sports Network.

Payton refocused again. No cracks in the rock, he found a handhold. No handholds, he used a daisy chain. No daisy chain, he went around the flat bastard. When one way up a mountain face didn't work, there was *always* another route.

Failure was not an option.

CHAPTER TWO

"PIT TIMES WERE GOOD."

"No. 467 car was all over me tonight…"

"No way."

"…track cooled down fast…"

Sound bites of conversation swirled around Rachel as she sat in the passenger seat and silently stared out the wet window. Although the sky had waited to open up and dump on them until after the race was finished, the heavy winds and lightning would've made flying home a nightmare. And since the motor-home drivers usually avoided traffic by taking off as soon as the races began, they had no place to stay at the track.

That had left only one option for a decent night's sleep; Hugo had called ahead for rooms at one of the hotels in the area that catered to NASCAR teams, and, wet and wired, the team had climbed into her uncle's rented Suburban.

"…yeah, but how'd the No. 414 car do?"

"Fourth."

"…springs might've been off…"

As the sun had set and the track had cooled down, Justin's No. 448 car had gotten loose. Fans loved the night races, with all the lights, the cool air and sparks flying, but they meant more guesswork for Rachel. With practice during the day and racing at night, the car adjustments tended to be a bit of a crapshoot.

"When's Dixon gonna fork out for a chassis simulator?"

"Ain't never gonna happen."

"His wallet's so tight, you can't squeeze a dollar bill *in*."

"Hey," Hugo cautioned. "No bad-mouthing the owner around me. You're all getting paid, aren't ya?"

Rachel didn't need a private company jet, but this wasn't the first time that Fulcrum owner Dixon Rogers's stingy habits had affected all of them. How'd he expect them to perform as well as the top teams when he refused to invest in additional research and development, or shell out for more wind tunnel time?

"Sixteenth is a respectable finish," her uncle said, "but we can do better."

Damn right they could do better. The last fifty laps of Justin positioning himself and then not having the power to make a move had about killed her. The urge to stomp her feet and throw her clipboard out the window overwhelmed Rachel. As usual, she stuffed it. Her uncle and the rest of the team didn't need her adding drama to the already disappointing finish.

They drove out of the rain and up to the hotel's main entrance. Justin and the rest of the team piled out of the rented SUV as Rachel cracked open her door.

Hugo stopped her with a hand on her arm and inclined his head. "Rachel, honey, you and Johnny got to work together figuring out what's wrong with that engine."

It's the exhaust manifold, she wanted to yell. She'd been trying to tell Johnny Meline, their engine builder, that NASCAR's Car of Tomorrow changes necessitated more modifications than Fulcrum had already made. Meline wouldn't listen to her.

"I know one day you want to be a good crew chief, but, remember, there's a lot more to it than the technical stuff," her uncle said without judgment. As stoic and distant as her uncle could sometimes be, he'd always been there for Rachel throughout her life, no matter what. The only way she knew how to repay him was to not cause him any more problems.

"I'll take care of it." Somehow. *On my own.*

She climbed out of the car, lost her balance on the rain-slicked pavement and tumbled right into... Whoa! Payton Reese. He must have been waiting for them at the hotel.

He reached out to steady her with arms as hard as rock and barely shifted with her weight. Rachel glanced into his cobalt-colored eyes. She hadn't noticed it before at the track, but his eyes were the exact deep blue of that classic Ferrari coupe Justin had been coveting. Only there was nothing steely about them. Confident to the point of cockiness, but not cold.

"You okay?" His hands, solid and warm, stayed on her arms until she righted herself.

"Thanks. I'm fine." When he let her go, she noticed a slight chill had settled in the wet night air and wished she could snuggle back up to all that heat.

Reporter, Rachel reminded herself. If not scum of the earth, he had to be darned close to it. All those people cared about were ratings and getting the nasty inside scoop on whatever story they were working on for that day, regardless of whether or not digging into the details messed with other people's lives.

"You guys ready to unwind?" Payton glanced from one team member to the next. "Hotel bar? Drinks are on me."

Figures. Rachel crossed her arms.

The others hooted and hollered.

"You got that right."

"Let's go."

"I like this man," Hugo said, tossing his keys to the valet. "He thinks like me."

They all headed into the hotel. Except Rachel. Maybe they wouldn't notice if she waited to check in until after they'd disappeared into the bar.

Payton held back. "Rachel, you coming?"

Hugo stopped and waved a hand, beckoning her along. "Come on, Rachel."

She shook her head. "You guys knock yourselves out. I'm bushed."

They all stopped and turned.

"Ah, Rachel."

"Have a beer."

"Just one."

She glanced from one pleading face to the next and stopped at too-good-looking-for-his-own-good Payton Reese. "Yeah, Rachel," he said with a grin. "Come play with us."

Smart aleck.

Justin waved everyone on and came back to where Rachel was standing.

"I saw that wink you gave everyone." She swatted him on the shoulder. "I'm tired. I want to go to my room."

Justin glanced behind him and presumably waited to talk until he'd assured himself they were alone. "I don't

see you complaining about being tired when your Flavor
of the Month is around."

"Flavor of the what?"

"You know. Like the country star wannabe that hung
around the tracks a while back. Those guys in and out—
mostly out—of your life. There was that history teacher
you met for a few weeks after work. Then military guy,
golf pro, bald pilot—"

"He was not bald."

Her brother raised his eyebrows at her.

"Okay, okay. Flavor of the Six Months, then."

"Whatever. My point is that when you meet people
after work everyone on the team notices."

She couldn't help but feel defensive. "What I do after
hours is my business. Not yours. Or anyone else's."

"I'm not trying to tell you who to date."

"Then what's this about?"

"Remember last month, when our PR rep asked a
group of us to go to Mooresville High School?"

As soon as he'd mentioned it, she'd found a reason to
leave the meeting early. Her stomach turned thinking
about it. All those teenagers in one spot, so eager to make
a connection, undisguised admiration oozing out of their
pores. She didn't want to be anyone's hero.

"I went, along with some guys on the pit crew, but they
needed you, Rachel. All the kids taking classes from their
shop department were there, including several girls. Like
it or not, you're a Murphy and a role model. People look
up to you."

"I don't have a responsibility to *people,* Justin. Pub-
licity is your department."

"You do have a responsibility to Fulcrum Racing.

We're a team. And teams do things together. It helps with morale and motivation." He shook his head. "When's the last time you had lunch with anyone at Fulcrum? Went out for a beer after work? Or hung out with the team and chitchatted?"

She usually brought her own lunches to work and ate in front of her computer while poring over car stats. Happy hours? She couldn't understand why anyone, after being forced to deal with the same people all day, would want to meet their co-workers again after hours. That was why she had her Flavors of the Month. And what would be the point in sitting around and *chitchatting?*

They were nice guys, but she liked her contained, insulated life. There was no room for the team in her world. Or anyone else for that matter. Her car had seats for three passengers, Hugo, Justin and her cousin Kim, Hugo's adopted daughter. And Rachel, not her brother, was behind the wheel.

"Come on, Rachel. It's Wade's birthday tomorrow." He tugged her along into the hotel. "One beer."

There was no doubt she had an advocate in Wade, so she supposed she could take a minor detour for the guy. "Oh, all right. One beer." She was probably too wired to sleep, anyway. "That's it." This was by no means becoming habitual.

After they'd all checked in at the front desk, she found herself at a big table in the bar sitting next to Payton, almost as if he'd planned it that way. Big surprise there. He probably wasn't even staying at this hotel.

A waitress, young and pretty, stopped by their table. "Two pitchers of beer, sweet thing," Dennis, her cousin, said with a wink and a smile. As usual, he flirted shamelessly, but there were times Rachel actually felt sorry for the guy, like tonight. He had no clue this blonde only had eyes for Justin.

After the drinks were delivered, they clanked their mugs together. "To next week. Darlington!"

Payton thanked everyone at the table for their help over the past weekend. He talked comfortably, telling jokes back and forth. Finally, inevitably, he leaned toward her. "You're awfully quiet. Tough race?"

The last thing she wanted to do right now was talk to a reporter. Not that she ever wanted to talk to a reporter. Ever again.

When she didn't respond, he held up his hands in mock surrender. "No camera. No notebook. Just making conversation. Promise."

She relaxed. A little. "Yeah, tough race."

"So Wade over there." He glanced toward the other side of the table. "I don't get how his job is different from Hugo's."

Puhleeze. Beer in hand, she glared at him, the NASCAR reporter who appeared to know nothing about NASCAR.

He laughed. "Go ahead. Say it. There's a smart remark dying for a breath of fresh air."

She smiled, couldn't help herself. She also couldn't seem to help noticing how his black hair curled a bit, how his tanned skin contrasted nicely with his white polo shirt.

"Let me try that again." He cleared his throat, all innocent. "What's the difference between a car chief and a crew chief?"

Oh, what the heck. "If sportscaster doesn't work out, you could always try weatherman. They usually don't know what they're talking about, either."

He chuckled. "I deserved that."

Rolling her eyes, she shook her head slowly back and forth. "Why NASCAR if you have no interest in racing?"

"Hey, this is my interview."

"You said no interview."

"I did, didn't I?" He sighed. "But saying I have *no* interest is extreme. I prefer to think of myself as a NASCAR virgin." His mouth barely curved, but his eyes sparkled with mischief. "Be gentle with me."

Heaven forbid, this guy wasn't so bad after all. Better to steer this conversation back to safer ground. "The crew chief's the boss. He works closely with the car chief in deciding what adjustments to make to the car before each race. The car chief and the rest of the team implement the changes the crew chief tells them to make."

He cocked his head, appearing genuinely interested in figuring it all out. "So Wade's your boss?"

"I report to our engine builder. Johnny Meline."

"Meline." He shook his head. "Why haven't I seen him around at the races?"

"He builds the engines at our facilities in Mooresville. He doesn't come to the tracks." The explanation almost stuck in her throat, and she was sure Payton noticed.

Before he could dig into that hornet's nest, she said, "Fulcrum has a lot of smaller teams that make up the whole crew. We have teams that travel and teams that stay at headquarters. A few of our people do both. Crew chiefs are in charge of everyone and the car. From the car's initial design to race-day strategies."

"Strategies?" His brow furrowed in concentration. "You're saying the driver doesn't get in the car and go as fast as he can for as long as he can?"

He might have said it with a smile, but he was obviously clueless. She shook her head, and he grew serious again. "I've been watching you guys for a few races now. You seem to do a lot more than most people on the Fulcrum team."

"I'm learning all the ropes." That, and she was an admitted perfectionist. She had a hard time relying on other team members.

"You want to be crew chief someday?"

He had no clue. When other high school girls had been dreaming of kisses and prom dresses, Rachel had been detailing out plans to become the first woman crew chief in NASCAR history. Someday, it was going to happen.

"Hey, Payton?" Hugo called across the table. "What'd you do before this sportscaster job?"

For the first time all night Rachel noticed the smile dim on Payton's face. "I was a mountain climber."

Was. Now there was a loaded three-letter word. No one else around the table seemed to catch it.

"You mean like Mount Everest?" Justin asked.

"Yeah, I've done Everest, but most of my ascents were more the technical, alpine-type climbing. Straight-up stuff."

And people thought NASCAR drivers were crazy.

"I did a documentary on my crew climbing one of the tallest peaks in South America," he continued. "A mountain called Cerro Torre. It was picked up by *National Geographic*. Kinda hit me with a filming bug. I want to do my own extreme sports show someday soon."

"So you hopped on the NASCAR bandwagon." Hugo nodded, but he didn't seem to mind. "Needing to make a name for yourself."

"Something like that."

"Smart move."

"Time will tell."

"So what was your hardest…?"

Perfect time to sneak away, while everyone was focused on Payton. Besides, she needed something other than beer to drink, and there wasn't a glass of water or a server in sight. Her cousin Dennis had probably scared the waitress away.

Without a word, she eased away from the table and went to the bar. After a few minutes, she figured, she could sneak away to her room and no one would be the wiser. Justin couldn't complain. She'd done her duty.

"Water, please?" she asked the bartender. A moment later, she felt movement of air and the warmth of a body next to her.

"Can I talk you into having dinner with me this week?"

Payton. His voice was so distinctive, it made heads turn. And listen. Resonant but soft, layered with tones of hot, lazy afternoons and dark, sexy nights. "I doubt it."

He chuckled, a sweet, syrupy sound settling warm in her stomach. "We can chat racing."

"I do that all day long." She turned toward him.

"Okay. All I've done is work since I moved here. You can show me around Charlotte."

She laughed.

"What?"

"How could one of North Carolina's ten most eligible bachelors not know a thing about Charlotte?"

He grinned. "When did you make that connection?"

"Back at the track. I read the article in the paper last week." She wouldn't tell him, heaven forbid, but he was even more virile in person than on TV or in his pictures. Not only did his face have the taut features of an athlete, but his body—his arms, his chest—oozed strength and power. The man had virtually no body fat.

For the second time that night he focused in on her neck and reached for the spot. "Grease." His hand stopped midair. "May I?"

Before she could say yes, his fingertips brushed her skin once. Twice. Too slowly. Or not slowly enough, she wasn't sure. She swallowed.

Instead of paying attention to what he was doing, he was staring into her eyes. "Do you like music?" The ever-present smile had disappeared from his face.

"Mmm-hmm."

"I do know this one place." He leaned his elbow onto the bar, bringing his face closer to hers, close enough that she could smell his cologne, a subtle but spicy scent. "Good food. The best jazz music in Charlotte—"

"You kids making some plans?" Hugo leaned against the bar next to Payton, his appearance not unlike shining a flashlight into a dark tunnel.

"I'm trying to—"

"No," she said, snapping to her senses. She pulled away from Payton and scowled a warning at her uncle. *Don't even think about it.* He was always setting her up in the hopes of getting her hitched.

Naturally, Hugo ignored her. "I've got two tickets to that new exhibition race at the dirt track outside Charlotte." He held them out. "Tuesday night."

Over the top of Payton's head, Rachel flashed her uncle another dirty look. No doubt he had good intentions, but she picked her own Flavors of the Month, as Justin had called them, and an appreciation for racing was a requirement. Except she loved dirt tracks, and her NASCAR schedule made it nearly impossible to attend the races held there primarily on Friday and Saturday nights.

And Hugo knew it.

"What kind of track?" Payton asked.

Rachel rolled her eyes. "It's dirt. And it's a race track."

Hugo chuckled. "No asphalt, Payton, makes for an interesting race. It's Rachel's favorite."

"What do you think?" Payton turned back toward her.

The man was sexy, she'd give him that.

"Go with Hugo." She slipped off the bar stool and headed to her room. "He likes you more than I do."

CHAPTER THREE

THIS WAS THE STUPIDEST thing Payton had ever set out to do. Even worse than free-climbing Devils Tower and definitely more dangerous. Unfortunately, it had seemed a good idea the other night in Richmond when Hugo had handed him one ticket to the dirt track and said, "Rachel will be there. I'll make sure of it."

Now, he was stuck. If he didn't show, he'd piss off a NASCAR icon. If he did, he'd piss off the icon's niece.

Probably better to take his chances with the niece.

Payton parked his car and his cell phone rang. The number displayed was his agent's. "Hey, Donna."

"How's it going?"

"The ball's rolling." Payton climbed out of his car and grimaced against a sudden stab of pain in his lower back. He hadn't been able to get in his regular workouts and stretches for the last several days, so his back was killing him. "My producer agreed to the NASCAR family specials. As soon as those air, we'll see what happens."

Jay Wilson had actually been ecstatic about the prospect of an interview with Rachel Murphy. That is, after he blew a gasket over Payton not having his special on the Murphy family ready to roll by the promised time. Payton had pacified him by telling him the Grosso family special would soon be ready to go, but he'd still given Payton only two weeks to get that interview with Rachel.

"Then I'll have something to take to the national networks," Donna said. "So make a statement with your NASCAR specials, Payton. Like you did with your climbing documentary. Stand out. Better yet, tie an improvement in your station's ratings to your NASCAR shows."

"I know, I know." Six months ago, she'd made the situation perfectly clear. The only way to get a national network to listen to Payton's pitch about his own extreme sports show was by making a splash in the world of sportscasting.

"I've put out a few feelers. There's definite interest out here."

"Then the rest is up to me."

"You got it. Keep me informed."

Payton stuffed his cell phone into the back pocket of his jeans, flipped on his sunglasses and entered the speedway with newfound purpose. He had to get that interview with Rachel.

While the announcers introduced the drivers, he bought a cold beer and walked toward the center of the bleachers. This time of night the sun was low on the horizon, but the sky was still clear and bright, so most of the fans wore sunglasses, hats or both. Row upon row of faces stared past him toward the track, and it was general admission. How was he supposed to find Rachel?

Front and center. Up a few rows, Hugo had said. *Rachel will be where the action is.*

The race would start any second. He caught himself searching for Rachel's Fulcrum baseball cap. Truth was, he had no clue what she looked like out of uniform.

Wouldn't mind finding out, though.

He climbed the steps higher than he thought she might sit and sat down in the first open aisle seat. There was no one immediately next to him, only a woman, facing away from him, down a few seats and several groups of mixed couples surrounding him. He studied the backs of the folks in the rows below him. A sea of solid-colored shirts and hats. If she was there, he'd have a hell of a time finding her.

He studied the woman in his row. She was wearing tight blue jeans and a pale green T-shirt and had long hair falling in loose curls past her shoulders. He couldn't see her eyes past the black wraparounds, or her face, angled as she was away from him, but there was something familiar—

Wait a minute. He watched her more closely. Similar hair color. Rachel?

Several folks in front of her turned around and chatted a few minutes. One of the guys handed her a fresh beer. *Naw. Not Rachel.* This woman was obviously with those people.

The exhibition race began and Payton found himself curious about what was happening. There weren't as many cars, and this track was much smaller than the others he'd seen, so it was easier to follow what was happening. The track looked wet, probably to keep the dust from flying, forcing the drivers to move much slower than on asphalt. As it was, the cars were sliding all over in the dirt, making the drivers slam and bump into one another.

A couple cars back from the lead, one driver cut in front of another, causing a small pileup. The men in front of Payton jumped up and yelled. Even the woman in his aisle stood up for a better look. This time Payton caught her profile. And that beautiful backside. It was Rachel.

He bought some hot dogs from a vendor and scooted down the aisle toward her. "I'm an idiot." He held out one hot dog. "Forgive me?"

She stared at him for a minute or two, as if she couldn't make up her mind. Finally, she shook her head and accepted the hot dog. "I don't know why it surprises me. My uncle does this kind of thing all the time."

"Let me guess. He told you he'd meet you here."

She nodded and took a bite of hot dog. "I'm going to kill him."

"At first, I didn't recognize you. Thought you were with these guys." He pointed to the group below them.

"They were asking some questions about the upcoming race at Darlington. *They* recognized me."

"So I've never seen you out of uniform." He shrugged. "You look…different." Gorgeous, is what he wanted to say.

She laughed at him. Laughed.

Could be worse. She could've taken it as an insult and gotten angry. "Sorry. It's your hair. I'm not used to seeing you without your baseball cap."

"You're forgiven." She grinned.

He tore his gaze away from her face and focused back on the track. "So who's your favorite driver?"

"You know, as much as we came to these tracks as a kid, I don't have time to follow this circuit anymore. I only recognize a few of the names." While keeping her eyes on the track, she explained the tactical differences of dirt versus short track versus superspeedway. It was all making some sense to him, and it was fun listening to the excitement in her voice, watching her watch the race.

"My dad started out racing dirt tracks," she said. "So did my uncle."

"Hugo used to drive?"

She looked at him quizzically and shook her head. "I don't know why I'm telling you all this."

"If I'm taking notes, you'll know it."

She thought about it for a few minutes, and then seemed to make up her mind. "The speed bothered Hugo, so he switched to working on the team. I've driven a few laps around the tracks here and there, too. I don't know how my brother does it. Did you ever get scared climbing?"

"Oh, yeah. The fear's always there. Between the heights and the elements, there's no rest for the wicked, as my mother would say. Nothing like getting literally picked up and tossed around by the wind a few times to keep you honest."

"You've been in winds that have picked you up? Your whole body?"

"The winds are strong on any mountain, but in the Patagonian range they gust to over 200 miles an hour. The locals call the winds there 'the Broom of God.'"

"That's kind of pretty."

"Scary is more like it."

"Why'd you keep doing it?"

He'd been asked that question so many times. He opened his mouth to give his pat answer and stopped. *Because I could* didn't seem fair. Or honest. "I don't know why. Why does Justin keep racing?"

She took her eyes off the track and studied him. "Racing seems safer."

"Only because you're familiar with it. I'd rather get hit by 200-mile winds than a 180-mile-an-hour car."

"You've got a point there." She chuckled. "Why climbing, though? That's not something you hear about every day."

He never told this story, but since he was being honest… "My dad died when I was twelve. Heart attack. Unexpected. I started having some problems in school." If you could count getting expelled as a problem. "Got into a few fights. Failed classes."

She flipped her sunglasses to the top of her head as if so she could listen better. The action only served to distract him, highlighting her long, thick hair, the freckles on her cheeks.

He looked away and went on. "My mom enrolled me in this outdoor program that included some climbing. Hanging out on the ropes at Yosemite turned me around. Mom promised me my own climbing equipment for staying out of trouble and finishing school. I had to work out, train, keep a schedule. It kept me focused. Before I knew it, the rush of it all was in my blood. I couldn't stop. It's what kept me feeling alive."

"That's what Justin says." She sighed. "I don't get it."

He shifted, stretched.

"Back bothering you?"

"It tightens up sometimes."

"Do you need to leave?"

"I'm fine." He didn't want to spoil her fun.

"Is your back why you don't climb anymore?"

Surprised, he said, "Who says I don't climb anymore?"

She didn't say anything. She didn't have to. She had the most expressive face he'd ever seen. "Okay, so I don't. And yeah, it's because of my back." He didn't want to go there with her. The wounds, both physical and mental, were still too fresh. "Want another beer?"

Understanding warmed the brown in her hazel eyes. "No, thanks."

They watched the race for a while longer, but the bleachers were killing him and he was having a hard time hiding that fact from Rachel.

"I'm getting tired," she said, stretching. The action drew her T-shirt taut over her chest, proving she'd been hiding a perfect—at least what he considered perfect—form under that brown-and-orange Turn-Rite uniform. "I think I'll be heading home."

"Your uncle said these dirt tracks were your favorite. Don't leave because of me. Please."

"It's been a long day." She stood. "Tomorrow will be longer."

He walked with her out to the parking lot and her truck, a new silver Chevy. "I know I'm pushing my luck, but will you have dinner with me tomorrow night? No Hugo this time."

She flipped her sunglasses back down. "Too busy this week getting ready for Darlington."

"Next week?"

She climbed in her truck, slammed the door and hung an arm out her open window. "I'll think about it."

"Don't think too hard," he yelled as she drove away.

He, on the other hand, had better think. Carefully. Being around Rachel was feeling less and less like work, and more and more like entertainment. That was definitely not a part of the plan.

RACHEL UNLOCKED the front door to her parents' house and stepped inside. No, not her parents' house. She turned the dead bolt, telling herself that she had to quit thinking of this property that way. Daddy and Mama had both been dead and gone close to thirty years. This was her house.

But was it *her* house yet?

It was late and dark outside, and the construction crew had long since gone home for the day, so she flicked on a light and walked around the day's mess they'd left behind. Another wall had been knocked down, and the kitchen countertops and the threadbare carpet from the dining room had finally been hauled away. Only a few original remnants of her parents' house remained.

Faded rose-print paper still covered the wall along the steps leading upstairs, steps she unaccountably remembered learning how to climb. The white linoleum with black flecks from her hazy childhood memories still covered the kitchen floor, its worn spots a clear reminder of where the red Formica table with matching vinyl chairs had sat for years.

All that, too, would be gone in a matter of a few days, at most a few weeks, and a sudden shock of panic raced through her.

What was she doing? She had no right to destroy her parents' house. She should be preserving what little was left of them. And this was it. This house. She had to put everything back. The furniture, the carpet, the walls.

Only there was nothing to put back. All that moth-eaten carpet and furniture was in the Dumpster out back, along with the curtains that had nearly disintegrated at the slightest touch and the mattresses that had been torn apart making room for squirrel or raccoon families.

Swallowing tears, she talked herself back to reality. There was something wrong about this place having sat empty all these years while she and Justin had lived with Hugo and Kim. What good had there been in letting this old house get overgrown with vegetation, cobwebs building upon cobwebs, the only inhabitants bats and rodents and ghosts from the past? Her parents were gone and there was nothing she could do to bring them back. At least now she was moving on.

Still shaking, Rachel made her way to the sliding doors leading out back and stepped onto the deck. The sun had long since set and the light of a low, full moon shone on the dark, glassy surface of Lake Norman.

The lake.

The truth was she'd hired a construction crew to redo the exterior of this old house. She'd replaced windows and the roof and slowly but surely they were transforming the interior, but no matter what she did or didn't do, this would always be her parents' home. This would always be her mother's lake.

Amidst the sound of crickets and the distant buzzing of cicadas, Rachel made her way to the shore and sat down in the wooden swing that had been her very first purchase after deciding to live here. It was an exact replica of the one she'd found rotting away in this very same spot. Kicking her foot into the dirt, she swung back and forth and uncovered some round, flat rocks, the kind perfectly shaped for skipping.

She scooped up a handful, went to the edge of the lake, wound back and tossed one out. She was rusty, but she threw out a few more and managed to skip several six or seven times over the smooth, black surface of the water. The sight and sound brought back memories of her, Justin and Kim hanging out at the beach when they were kids, the feeling of the sand between her toes and sunshine on her shoulders.

"Sure, Rachel. Don't worry about it."

She drove the modified golf cart as close to Payton as she could get. "Come on. Let's get you someplace quiet."

He tried to straighten and stopped, grimacing.

"Can you lean on me? Somehow?"

Now his breaths were short, almost pants. "My left side is better."

She scooted next to him and wrapped her arms around his waist. As she'd guessed, rock-hard muscles lay under that warm layer of skin. *Oh, man.* "Come on. This isn't the time for the tough-guy act." He slumped against her. "Can you walk?"

"Barely. Pain's shooting down my legs." He shuffled to the cart, and she helped lower him onto the seat. "Where are we going?" he whispered, as if talking normally hurt too much.

She eased the foot pedal down so as not to jerk him around. "Hugo's coach."

"His what?"

"Motor home. In the owners' and drivers' lot. Rather than a hotel, I usually stay with him at the tracks."

She checked in at the security gate, and they didn't have far to go. Her uncle's motor home was parked right next to Justin's aluminum, bullet-shaped monstrosity. She parked the club car and quickly went to Payton's side. This time he had no problem leaning on her. When they got to the steps, she paused. There were no handrails. "This won't be easy."

The door opened and Kim came outside. "Whoa," she said. "Strange welcoming committee. Need some help?"

"Yeah, but I'm not sure what you can do."

"You pull. I'll push. If I have to."

Rachel managed to bend over and let Payton use her body to leverage himself up the steps. Kim stayed behind and made sure he didn't fall backward. Rachel helped him back to the bedroom she shared with Kim when her cousin was able to make the races, and eased Payton down to a sitting position on the mattress.

"Kim, this is Payton Reese. He's a sportscaster for WJAZ."

"Hey, Payton. I've caught your race coverage a few times. For a California boy, you do okay."

"Payton, this is Kim. Hugo's daughter."

"Hi, Kim," Payton said, smiling weakly. "I'd interview you, but…"

"Where are those darned cameramen when you need them?" Kim said, smiling.

A sense of humor and attractive. Maybe Hugo should've set Payton up with Kim.

For the first time since they'd been kids, Rachel felt insecure in her cousin's presence. With Kim's classic features, blond hair and translucent gray eyes, it'd been no surprise growing up that she'd been the princess and Rachel the tomboy. Kim, though, had always been completely unaware of her beauty, so Rachel did her best to squelch the anxiety. One word from Rachel, and Kim would steer herself hundreds of miles from Payton.

"You okay for a minute?" Rachel asked Payton. "I'll go get something for the pain."

"Sure."

"I'll make sure he doesn't fall over," Kim said.

Worst case, Rachel would have to go to the track medic, and then she remembered Hugo having some problems with his back once at a race. They'd given him muscle relaxants, which were bound to help spasms. She found them in the bathroom cabinet and grabbed a bottle of water from the fridge before heading back to her bedroom.

"Can you sit up and swallow pills?" She held Payton with one arm and handed him the medicine.

"What is it?"

"Muscle relaxant."

After he'd downed a dose, Rachel said, "One more thing." Running to Justin's trailer, she raided his stash of heating pads and ran back to Payton. "I have heating pads. What position is most comfortable?"

"On my side."

She and Kim helped him position himself, plugged in two pads and covered his back. "Will that work? Payton?"

"Thank you…Rachel."

"What am I, chopped liver?" Kim whispered.

Within minutes, Payton was sound asleep. Kim motioned toward the living room. "I'll wait out there."

CHAPTER FIVE

RACHEL SAT ON THE BED a minute longer and took her time studying Payton's still form, the corded length of his arms, the steady rising and falling of his chest. Fit, rock hard and muscular. It seemed strange for such a powerful man to be brought down, made this vulnerable. If this had been due to a fall, it'd been a bad one.

Slowly, the lines on his face cleared and his jaw relaxed. His mouth turned slack and she wondered how those lips would feel. Another place. Another time. Maybe. Maybe not. It was too soon to call it.

After easing off his shoes, she closed the blinds and turned on the overhead fan to help him stay cool. Then she tiptoed out and closed the door.

Kim was sitting on the couch with a satisfied grin on her face. "I'm telling Daddy you brought a man back to his motor home."

"And make his day. Why would you want to do that?"

Kim laughed. "Did he set you two up?"

Rachel explained what happened at the dirt track. "Payton's actually a pretty decent guy."

"If you don't want him, I'll take him."

Kim and Payton would no doubt make a cute pair. A twinge of possessiveness swept through Rachel, but she stuffed it. "Knock yourself out."

"Hmm." Kim grunted. "I'll wait and see."

"Suit yourself." Rachel filled a cooler with refreshments. "You feeling okay?" Her cousin's attendance at races had been sporadic lately, and over the past few months Kim had lost weight. She said it was stress, and no matter how much the family pushed, she refused to see a doctor.

"I'm fine. What're you doing with that cooler?"

"Taking some sodas back to the garage."

"Nursing a sick guy. Drinks for the team. What's gotten into you?"

"I can be as motherly as the next guy."

"Exactly."

Rachel chuckled. "Justin gave me an all-for-one-and-one-for-all speech in Richmond."

"And you bought it?"

"He was fairly persuasive."

"I'll take it to the garage." Kim grabbed the cooler. "You have some lunch and take care of Mr. Hunka Burning Back Pain."

"Thanks, Kim. Can you take the club car back to Paul?"

"Will do."

Rachel made herself a turkey sandwich with mustard and Swiss cheese. Unsure what Payton might eat, she made the same thing for him. She looked at the time. He'd been resting with those heating pads for almost an hour. Surely long enough, if not too long. After raiding the supply of cold packs from her brother's trailer, she eased open her bedroom door.

Immediately, his eyes flickered open. "Hi," he breathed. "Have I been out long?"

"About an hour. We should switch you to ice packs."

"Good idea." He moved tentatively, testing his back.

"How's it feel?"

"Not too bad. Thanks to you."

"Let me get those off."

As she leaned over him to remove the heating pads, he brushed his hand along her arm. "Thank you," he murmured.

The motion seemed innocent enough, but it still threw Rachel off, heightening her awareness of him in these small quarters. "No problem. Did you want the cold packs on right away?"

"Please."

"Where do you want them?"

"Around the middle."

She arranged the packs around the center of his back, and kept them in place while helping him sit up. "I made you something to eat, if you're hungry." She went out to the kitchen and brought back the sandwich.

"Thank you." He accepted the paper plate. "I might've passed out if you hadn't come by." He took a couple bites and a swig of water.

She sat down on the edge of the bed. "How did you do this to your back?"

"On a climb. Before Christmas. About six months ago."

"What happened?"

"Pretty foolish stuff. My partner wasn't taking in the rope. When I fell there happened to be too much slack. And a ledge with my name on it several feet below me. I hit the rock. Perfectly. On my back. Smashed three vertebrae."

She cringed. "You could've been paralyzed."

"Funny you should say that." He chuckled. "I couldn't walk for two months."

"So now you can walk, but the pain knocks you down."

"I haven't figured out a good out-of-town exercise

routine, and if I don't work out and stretch, the muscles tighten. Then they spasm. And then you see me in this shape."

"There's a workout facility here in the motor-home lot. I'll get you passes so you could use that if you wanted."

"The drivers work out here? At the tracks?"

"Don't tell me you're one of those people who think NASCAR drivers aren't athletes?"

"Okay, I won't." His back must be feeling better. He was grinning again. "Thanks for the book, by the way."

"What book?" She tried acting innocent, but acting anything had never been her strong suit.

He wasn't biting. "Let's just say this dummy's learning a lot about NASCAR."

"You're welcome." She couldn't keep a smile from cracking. "Where'd this happen? Your fall?"

"Ha! That's the really funny part." He chuckled again, this time a hollow, edgy sound. "I've climbed all over the world. Never got hurt. Nepal, Bolivia, Russia. Made some of the most difficult ascents on some of the most difficult mountains in the world. And what do I do? Almost die on El Cap in Yosemite. Home turf. A climb I could do in my sleep."

She shook her head. "And yet you want to keep doing it? These climbing expeditions?"

"Not exactly. I'll be filming them."

"But you'll still be climbing."

He studied her, his smile slowly disappearing. "Some of it."

"Why?" She couldn't help it, couldn't keep the incredulity out of her voice. "Why would you risk your life? Risk walking?"

He glanced at her, eyes full of uncertainty. "Most people don't get it."

"Try me."

He looked away. "I told you my dad died of a heart attack, right? He was only forty-two. My grandpa died at thirty-six. Great-grandpa at thirty-eight. And many of the other men in my family, uncles, cousins, have all died of heart disease or something else as serious around forty."

"That's crazy." She felt her jaw drop, couldn't help it. "How old are you?"

"Thirty-two. A ticking bomb."

"Did they have any other health issues?"

"They were all overweight. Just because I'm not, doesn't mean I can sit back and relax. I have two younger brothers watching and waiting to see what happens to me. I'd rather show them a man who hasn't given in."

"A man who'd rather die climbing."

"Flat on my back on the living room floor is no way to go."

She considered the pain etched in his face. "You found your dad, didn't you?"

He nodded. "I tried pumping his chest, giving him mouth-to-mouth, like I'd seen on TV." He paused, taking a deep breath, remembering. "It seemed like forever before the ambulance got there, and when they did, they said he'd been long gone. There was nothing I could've done."

"How's your heart?"

"As healthy as an eighteen-year-old's, but I won't be slacking off."

"Fighting it every step of the way." She didn't honestly blame him.

"You got it," he said with a grin. "I think it's time for some heat." He meant heating pads, but the mischievous glimmer in his eyes made her wonder.

"What kind of heat?" She couldn't help herself.

He picked up her hand and brought the inside of her wrist to his mouth. "Mmm, the smell of Lava's starting to turn me on."

She giggled, but her belly warmed like those heating pads. "The climbing walls I've seen look challenging. You know, in gyms and sporting stores."

"Those are boring. I'll take you climbing on the real thing."

"Like Yosemite? Not a chance."

"There are lots of smaller climbs all over the country. You've got a few out your back door."

"Where?"

"Crowders Mountain, for one. Not all that far from Charlotte." He rubbed the inside of her wrist. "I'll take you, if you're interested."

"Why would I want to try something that almost paralyzed you?"

"This is top roping. Much safer than lead climbing. Easy stuff. And you'd be good at it."

She had to admit she was curious. "How do you know?"

"The way you move. Your balance. Your strength."

She'd never thought of herself as strong, but attempting something so different, something she'd never before considered, held definite appeal. "You really think I could do it?"

"I know you could."

She tried to imagine herself on a rock face. "Forget it."

"Scared?"

"Yeah."

He was silent for a moment. "Dinner, then?"

That was possible, although it meant moving into Flavor of the Month territory. Payton certainly fit the bill. His NASCAR stint was temporary, so she wouldn't have to worry about him overstaying his welcome. No one would ever mistake this action-loving California boy for the type to get serious and settle into a quiet Southern lifestyle.

Normally, she'd be jumping all over this guy. Why the hesitation?

Maybe it was time for something new. A Flavor of the Month with a Twist.

"I'm sick of flings, Payton. I've had enough of them over the years. What I could use is a friend."

Another few minutes of silence passed while he seemed to consider her offer. "I can live with that." He finally smiled, a bit lopsided. "No date. Dinner. Friends it is."

"How does Tuesday sound?"

"I'll pick you up."

"The roads around Lake Norman can get confusing," she said, not wanting him to come to her house. That place was filled with too much emotion right now for her, and she wasn't sure she wanted to open that door. "There's a strip mall parking lot off Highway 77, exit 150. I'll meet you there. Six o'clock."

CHAPTER SIX

A DATE. What had he been thinking?

Rachel could call it anything she wanted, but a man and woman going out for dinner was, by any other name, a *date*.

Payton studied the directions Rachel had e-mailed him earlier in the day and gave a half second's thought to turning back to Charlotte. Saying he'd gotten lost would've been a long shot, but, any way you looked at it, not too far off the mark.

He'd gotten off track all right. Hadn't he promised himself no women, no attachments, not even one-nighters before he'd taken this North Carolina gig? Work, work and more work.

Maybe she was right. He had to quit thinking about tonight as a date. This was all about figuring the woman out and getting her more comfortable around him. And hopefully the camera.

The parking lot off exit 150 where she said she'd meet him was easy to find. Rachel, on the other hand, was nowhere to be found, but he was early. He found a spot where she could easily see him from the road, rolled down his windows and turned off his engine.

He'd no sooner taken out his PDA to go through a few

e-mails than a vehicle drove alongside him. Rachel, still dressed in her Fulcrum uniform, rolled down her window.

"You're a little early, and I'm a lot late," she said. "Sorry. Had some problems at work."

"Don't worry about it. Wanna reschedule?"

She hesitated, considering it. "If you don't mind following me home, it'll only take me fifteen minutes to shower and change."

Fifteen minutes. He chuckled, never having known a woman who could get ready for anything in twice the time. "We're not in any rush. I'll follow you."

She drove out of the parking lot and headed west on county road 150. In a short time, they'd left Mooresville stoplights and traffic congestion behind for roads heavily wooded with longleaf pine, oaks and red cedars and dotted with flowering dogwood.

Shortly after crossing an area where Lake Norman was visible on either side of the road, Rachel took a left onto a newly paved road. Small developments of brand-new homes with perfectly manicured yards bordered the drive. After catching a glimpse of several homes surrounding a small bay, he figured this had to be one of Lake Norman's countless peninsulas. The lots were large and sloped gently down to the lake's edge where any number of pontoons and speedboats were docked.

As they approached what appeared to be the end of the road, a gated entrance appeared. She drove past the Private Property signs posted on several large cottonwoods, through an open steel gate and onto a narrow dirt path. After what might have been apple or peach orchards, the old trees either neglected or dead, they headed into several hundred yards of heavy woods. When he thought they had to be close to hitting water, the road ended in a circular driveway. He pulled up by the three-car garage behind Rachel's truck.

The property wasn't merely located at the end of the peninsula, she owned most of the peninsula. Maybe the privacy factor had something to do with her wanting to meet at the parking lot off the highway exit.

He let it go. None of his business.

To the left, a Strom Construction pickup was parked next to two other cars and ahead on the eastern shore, a modest redbrick house with fresh white shutters and trim and a steeply sloped roof was nestled within a grove of old oaks, pines and other hardwoods. The place looked brand-new except that the trees seemed old, mature, as if their roots had been in that ground for hundreds of years. Landscaped to perfection, this place could have come right out of a home magazine.

"I'll be damned," he muttered to himself. She didn't exactly project a Susie Homemaker image at the track.

Only there was something missing. Color. Except for the actual house and a few poorly trimmed crepe myrtles lining one side of the yard, the place was nothing but variations of green. Then again, who was he to criticize? Mr. Homemaker he was not.

Through his open window, he heard her car door slam and climbed out of his car. Behind dark sunglasses, he studied the way the browns and oranges of the uniform complemented her features, bringing out the green in her hazel eyes and a sunny tone to her skin.

"Come on in. It'll take me fifteen minutes. I swear."

He followed her onto a wide front porch, a porch that was entirely barren, but for what looked like a week old county paper, waterlogged and yellowed by the sun. "Did you build this place?"

"Nope. It's my parents' old house." She shook her head, and he caught a whiff of engine grease coming off her clothes and hair. He was getting used to that smell. "After they died, Hugo couldn't get himself to sell the property. He decided to hold on to it until Justin and I were old enough to make up our own minds. Last summer, we finally got around to checking things out and found the structure was still surprisingly sound."

That was probably the most he'd heard her say at one time. This house must be a big deal to her. "Bet the grounds were overgrown."

She rolled her eyes and shook her head. "You have no idea. There was so much underbrush we could barely make it to the front door. After hauling all of that out of here, the contractors replaced the roof and refurbished the exterior. Now, we're working on the inside. It should be completely finished in another month or so."

"Racing must pay pretty well."

"It's better if you're winning. Big." She laughed. "I don't make enough yet to pay for all this work, and all my savings are going for furniture." She flicked her hand at the house. "But the property was owned free and clear, so I took out a mortgage to cover the construction."

"This kind of secluded property on Lake Norman's worth enough, that's for sure."

"That's why we decided to keep it." She nodded, glancing into the tall treetops. "Split the peninsula down the middle. I took this side and Justin will eventually settle permanently on the undeveloped side."

"When he gets married?" Payton might not know

much about the details of racing NASCAR, but he was getting to know the personalities. He took a chance and decided to test the waters. "You may find yourself living next to a Grosso."

"Not if I have anything to say about it."

Not too happy about her brother's relationship with Sophia Grosso. That surprised him. By all accounts, the Murphy siblings were close and the old Hatfield and McCoy feud seemed archaic.

She opened the front door, a heavy old solid wood thing, with ornate carvings and an oval leaded-glass insert. Exactly the kind of thing Payton's own mother would've stocked in her antique store back in San Francisco.

The house had been completely gutted and was in the process of being rebuilt. Plywood, drywall, trim, tools and sawhorses were scattered everywhere. And every flat surface was covered in a fine layer of dust and wood shavings.

"Hey, there, Rachel." A balding man with a leather tool belt strapped around his slight middle-aged paunch stepped toward them from what would someday be a kitchen. "You're home early."

"And you guys are working late."

"Have to do that now and again if you want us finished by the Fourth of July."

"Harlan, this is Payton Reese. Payton, this is Harlan Strom. He's the contractor in charge of the construction out here and a good friend of Hugo's."

They shook hands, and the man's eyes widened in recognition. He pointed at Payton's chest. "You're the new sportscaster on Channel Eleven, aren't you?"

"Yep."

"I knew it." Harlan smiled and glanced at Rachel. "Um…we were finishing for the day." Two young men nodded their hellos and goodbyes as they stepped past them and headed for their cars. "Should have the kitchen almost done by late next week. Oh, and you need to decide on paint."

"Didn't I already do that?"

"Couldn't decide between Tansy Green or Ecru, remember?"

She looked to Payton.

"Uh-uh." He held up his hands. Him and home decor went together about as well as ice picks and granite.

"Green," she said.

Harlan nodded, acting as if there was something he needed to say, but didn't know how to broach the topic. Rachel, clearly not picking up the man's signals, flipped through her mail. Finally, Harlan said, "Well, I'll get out of your way."

"Thanks, Harlan. See you later." She closed the front door behind him and then pointed Payton lakeside. "There's a refrigerator over there. Help yourself to whatever. I'll be right back."

Payton stepped over the clutter lying on the floor and made his way toward the back of the house. Everything was in a state of flux, some things finished, others torn apart. New kitchen cabinets had been installed, but there were no countertops, let alone a sink. He opened the brand-new refrigerator, grabbed a bottle of water and glanced at the one and only picture hanging on the wall.

It seemed out of place, neatly hung in a house all torn apart. Rachel, Justin, Hugo and Kim, Hugo's adopted daughter, whom he vaguely remembered from Darlington. Strange that Rachel could handle a house all torn apart, but she wanted her family front and center.

Payton, on the other hand, hadn't even talked to his mom for close to three months and hadn't seen his sister and two younger brothers since they'd visited him in the hospital after his accident. There'd been no falling-out, or anything quite so dramatic. Losing contact with his family was more a casualty of his lifestyle than anything, a casualty with which he'd long ago come to terms.

He turned to one of several sliding-glass doors opening to a long, wide deck. He stepped outside and stretched his back while studying the yard. Once again, he couldn't help but notice the absence of color. Everything was immaculately landscaped, but there were no flowers or flowering shrubs. The backyard was green upon green upon more green.

Thick, wild woods surrounded the property on either side. Several large trees shaded the house and lawn and provided plenty of privacy. A narrow grassy area sloped down to Lake Norman, where the early-evening sun sparkled on the water's calm surface. Next to a wide dock, a pontoon was housed and near the water's edge, under the shade of a huge willow, hung a double swing from a thick log frame.

This property was so secluded, there wasn't even a distant noise of traffic. The only sound he could hear was the cooing of a mourning dove from its perch in the long branches of a nearby magnolia. Payton closed his eyes for several minutes and felt all his remaining tension float away on the cool breeze blowing in off the lake.

"Peaceful, isn't it?"

He looked at his watch and smiled. Fifteen minutes, practically on the nose. He should have figured as much from an engineer.

When he spun around, he couldn't keep his eyes from opening wide. If Rachel at the race the other night in jeans and a T-shirt had been a surprise, Rachel in a dress was something altogether amazing. She wore most of her hair down with only a few chunks tacked up with some kind of pins, giving the style a flirty feel. Her dress was a clingy halter-top thingy in a bold sixties-type pattern in greens, browns and oranges. The hemline didn't quite reach her knees, and he couldn't help but notice she had the prettiest ankles he'd seen in a long time.

"You look…gorgeous." He went ahead and said it.

"Here we go again." She grinned, her mouth glossy with, of all things, lipstick. As an engine specialist, he'd taken her for a tomboy. How wrong could one man be?

He leaned against the deck rail and decided a change in subject was best. "This is quite a home."

"I was born here." She joined him on the deck. "I mean, my parents were living here when my brother and I were born."

"You were pretty young when your parents died, weren't you?"

She nodded. "Not quite two when my mom…when she…died. It wasn't long after that when my dad was killed."

Talk about over-the-top tragedy in one person's life. "Do you remember either of them?"

"A little. From this house." A memory passed over her features before she straightened her shoulders. "Should we go?"

The drive to Charlotte went by in a heartbeat, filled as it was by their conversation. Their first stop was a well-known bistro in the heart of the city's historic South End district, a cozy, casually upscale restaurant with white linen tablecloths and hardwood floors. Beyond hot dogs and beer, he had no idea as to her tastes.

"I've never been here before," he admitted. "You?"

"Nope. But I love food."

"Let's hope it's good." He ordered tenderloin with some sauce, the ingredients for which he didn't attempt to pronounce, and she couldn't decide between the pork medallions and the day's special, crab-stuffed grouper.

"Get the special," he said. "We'll come back another time for the pork." The suggestion had no sooner left his mouth than he wanted to bite it back. Another time implied another *date*.

"Good idea." She surprised him by agreeing, and, when the fish came to their table, it was so tasty she gave him a small sample. "For future reference purposes," she said. After the meal and another glass of chardonnay, she wasn't saying much. Either she was full and content, or something was on her mind.

Her face gave everything away. "Come on. Out with it. I can see those questions building inside your mouth like cars piling up on a race track."

"As if you'd know a pileup from a setup." She smiled and leaned her elbows onto the table. "How come you're not married?"

Married. The word alone sent a blip of cold fear through his veins. The memory of his dad lying dead on the living room carpet, his face pale and lifeless, flashed through him. That was never going to happen to Payton.

There'd be no slipping quietly into oblivion for him, not if he had anything to say about it. When he died, he was going out with a bang, on a mountain face somewhere doing what he loved best.

"That's easy." He shook it off and smiled at Rachel. "For the last decade I've done at least one climbing expedition every year. They take a lot of planning, and I was on the road a lot." He glanced at her. "You know a woman who can handle her man gone for six months out of every year?"

She shook her head. Both of them knew there was no such person.

"There you go," he said. "I've never found a woman who could make settling down sound like anything better than settling for less."

"That's harsh."

"But true." And she knew what he was talking about. While doing his research, he'd heard about all the various men in her life, but not one serious or long-term relationship. "How come you're not hooked up?"

"Who says I'm not?"

"We wouldn't be out tonight if you were." He chuckled. Not a date. Yeah, right. "There's not a man alive who'd let a woman like you go out to dinner with a guy, one-on-one, friends or not."

"You think it's only women who have problems with their significant others being gone all the time? Think again." She shook her head. "The NASCAR season is long and hard. I wouldn't know a Monday through Friday, forty-hour workweek, if it jumped up and bit me in the butt. Ever met a man who could stand his girlfriend heading out of town forty weekends out of every year?"

"They gotta be out there."

"Maybe, but I can guarantee there isn't a man out there who'll put up with being second place in a woman's life. I want to be a crew chief more than a girlfriend or wife." She shook her head. "No attachments. Keeps things simple."

Finally, a woman who understood. Maybe this NASCAR stint wouldn't be so bad after all. "Tell me you dance, Rachel."

CHAPTER SEVEN

HARLAN STROM LEFT the construction mess behind at Rachel's house, pulled into a drive-through, ordered a bunch of burritos and a taco salad and, as an afterthought, added a few cartons of milk. He took off toward home, a sick feeling settling in his gut. Catie would be waiting for him, dying for some news, and he'd be disappointing her again.

He pulled into the driveway to their modest split-level and, as usual, the garage door was open, the hood on that old car she'd been restoring for the past year was propped open and rock music blared from the workbench radio. A pair of legs, clad in holey, faded jeans, stuck out from under the old car and the attached sneakered feet kept some semblance of time with the music, if you could call it that. The next-door neighbor kid, Derek Weaver, was leaning over the engine and looked over as Harlan put her in Park.

He climbed out of his truck, walked into the garage and snapped off the radio. "Derek." He nodded at the young man in a black T-shirt with the sleeves torn off and the word *Nirvana* printed on the front.

"Hey, Mr. Strom."

Harlan set the fast-food bag on the workbench, dug out two burritos and handed them to Derek. "You hungry?"

"Yes, sir. Thank you."

Either teenagers were bottomless pits, or Derek's mama never fed that boy. Then again, there was another possibility. The kid spent so much of his time hanging around the Strom house that his mama never had much of a chance to feed him.

Harlan tossed the kid a carton of milk. Derek grimaced slightly, but drank it anyway. Good kid.

"Hey, you." Harlan tapped one of his daughter's beat-up sneakers. "Supper's here."

"What did you get?" Catie slid out from under the car and wiped her greasy hands off on a rag sticking out of her back pocket.

"Taco salad."

She scrunched her face in a way only a fifteen-year-old could manage. "We had Mexican last night."

He dug back into the bag and handed her the plastic take-out container. "Don't like it, learn to cook."

That's what young women were supposed to be doing, anyway. Cooking, giggling, primping their nails and hair. Going on dates. They sure as hell weren't supposed to rebuild engines on old classic cars, Harlan thought to himself.

"I hate being in the kitchen." She leaned against the fender and dug into the salad with a plastic fork. "Mexican it is."

"And drink this." He tossed her some milk.

She rolled her eyes at him.

"Young women need calcium." At least that's what Harlan had heard.

"Yum." She laughed at Derek, but drank it anyway.

With that cheerful personality, she ought to be able to get a boyfriend. She was pretty enough, that wasn't the problem. Sure, he was biased, being her father and all, but he'd noticed the way boys looked at her when they went to church, or out to dinner, and she'd left her long blond hair down instead of tied up in that infernal ponytail. Problem was, Catie didn't give a hoot. All she cared about was this car.

Harlan shook his head and took a bite of his own burrito. He had no one to blame but himself. He should've gotten remarried after Lynette died. Little girls didn't deserve being brought up by some burly construction-minded man. They needed their mamas. A slurp of milk cleared the beans and rice that seemed to catch in his throat. What did he know about sleep-overs and diaries, stylish clothes and eye shadow? No wonder Catie preferred screwdrivers to hair dryers and 10W40 to perfume. Cars to boys. She'd be turning sixteen soon, and it was clear he'd made some mistakes along the way.

Catie raised her eyebrows at him. "I'll bet Rachel Murphy doesn't cook."

Rachel Murphy had never had a serious boyfriend, either.

"I get my license soon, Daddy." Catie pushed around her lettuce leaves, and he braced himself for the inevitable. "Did you ask her?"

Harlan looked away from the expectation in her beautiful brown eyes, eyes that reminded him so much of Lynette it nearly broke his heart.

"You didn't, did you?" Her shoulders slumped and she set the salad down.

"We'll figure it out," Derek said.

Harlan barely heard him. "Sweetie, Rachel's a busy woman."

"But you're at her house almost every day," Catie said. "How hard can it be to ask her one simple question?"

"She's not there most of the time. You know that."

"You've been working out there for months. I'm not stupid. I know what's going on." Catie shook her head and tears welled in her eyes. "Come on, Derek. Let's get out of here." Right before slamming the door heading into the house, she yelled, "You just don't want me to finish this car."

No. That wasn't it at all. But damned if Harlan could figure out what *was* bothering him.

RACHEL AND PAYTON FOUND a club not too far away from the restaurant with a live jazz band. The old place with brass fixtures and intricate wrought-iron railings had a New Orleans kind of feel, comfortable, casual and sultry. When Payton started for the bar, Rachel yanked him in the other direction—right onto the dance floor.

The action was so unlike anything she'd ever done she didn't know what to think. Was it the music and its smooth, contagious beat, the bottle of wine they'd shared at the restaurant, or simply being around Payton? There was no doubt she felt comfortable with him, as if she could talk about anything.

"I'm guessing you don't get much of a chance to dance at the race tracks," he said, slowly turning her around.

"Or you in the mountains."

One slow song led to another and whatever had gotten into Rachel started feeling real good. Payton's arms fit perfectly around her, and his hands warmed her hips and her back through the thin, clingy fabric of her dress. She couldn't decide what felt better: his hands on her, or her hands on him. Finally, she stopped questioning herself and what might or might not happen and let the sensations flow.

After a pause in sets, she ran her hands up the front of his pale gray dress shirt. The solid mass of his muscles beneath the crisp, smooth cotton was a delightful contrast. "How often do you work out?"

"Every day." His gaze moved from her eyes to her lips and back again.

"Isn't that hard on your injury?"

"It's the only thing that keeps me limber, keeps the muscles from tensing." The music began again, and he drew her close. "Work out with me sometime," he whispered in her ear.

"Me?" She laughed. She had to. His breath on her neck practically turned her to jelly. Good thing he was holding her up. "I've never exercised a day in my life."

"All the running around at the track must keep you in shape." He tightened his grip at the small of her back, almost lifting her onto him. "You feel great."

Suddenly, those sensations were flowing all too well. If they didn't stop right now, she might follow through with the urge to lift her legs and wrap them around his waist.

She pulled back. "I think we should go."

"All right." He seemed shaken, as if she'd broken a spell. In a way, she supposed, she had.

The walk back to his car proved awkward and quiet, and she regretted ruining the night. Once they were on the road and driving back to her house, she tried lightening the mood. "Have you gotten to know the area at all?" she asked. Before long they were talking about activities in and around Charlotte. "Headquarters for several of the top racing teams are in the area," she reminded him. "Any self-respecting NASCAR reporter has toured several of them."

"I promise to hit one a week until I've covered them all." He smiled then grew serious as he pulled into her driveway. "I'm sorry if I got carried away back at the club—"

"Don't," she said. "It was me, not you."

They climbed out of his car. As he walked her across the driveway and down the winding sidewalk, crickets chirped their nighttime welcome. "Want to check out the lake?" he asked.

A part of her didn't want the night to end, either, but the lake was off-limits. "I don't think so," she said, trying to keep the answer from sounding like a door slamming shut.

From the look in his eyes, she had a feeling she didn't succeed. At the front steps, she faltered. "Well…"

"Thanks for the company, Rachel. I haven't danced in a long time."

"Me, neither."

"Not a date," he said, as if he were reminding himself and not her.

She stepped away, and he touched her hand. Barely, but that's all the invitation she needed. She turned back around and walked into his arms. And stayed there. A minute. Maybe two. In a hold too intimate to be called a hug.

He leaned his forehead against hers. "What are we doing, Rachel?"

She wished she knew. "Could be this is all about you wanting an interview."

"Maybe the night started out that way." Slowly, he shook his head. "Right now an interview is the furthest thing from my mind."

"In that case, we're having fun." She offered the best answer she had. "Enjoying each other's company. Is there a problem with that?"

"Absolutely not. As long as we both know where we stand."

"We stand as friends. This is casual. No ties, no expectations, no commitments. No claims. We might sleep together. We might not. It's too soon to tell."

"I've never met a woman who could live with that. You think you can?"

"I'm sure. Can you?"

"Yes, ma'am." Already, he was sounding a bit Southern, but the intensity of his gaze was anything but polite. "Give me the contract and I'll sign it right now. Tonight. Then we can take care of that sleeping together part you mentioned."

"Too soon for a first date, isn't it?"

"I thought we agreed this wasn't a date."

She leaned in, bent her nose against his, brushed her mouth over his. He brushed back. She tasted her own lip gloss on him. Red raspberry, sweet and a little tangy.

"I suppose that wasn't a kiss," he murmured.

"Not by a long shot."

But it had been the most moving not-a-kiss on such a comfortable not-a-date she'd ever experienced. She nearly changed her mind and walked down with him to the lake. A definite no-no.

Instead, she looked into his eyes, tilted her head and opened her mouth over his. He was as sturdy as a wall, and she melted into him, running her tongue along his with motions that were as much a dance as the moves they'd made at the club earlier. He moved to wrap his arms around her, but she drew away.

"*That* was a kiss." She ran up the steps and into her house, closing the door firmly behind her. As flavors went, Payton Reese was proving to be sweet as could be.

CHAPTER EIGHT

"THE CAR'S STILL not running right." Justin's voice sounded scratchy over the headset.

"What exactly is the problem?" Rachel asked, frustrated.

"I don't know!"

Her little brother sounded a little pissed at her. Too bad. If they couldn't identify the issue, she couldn't fix it. This was the last of their practice runs around the Charlotte speedway before the race and their last shot to make adjustments.

"Loose? Tight?" Wade asked.

"It's not the suspension," Justin said. "I can't get any speed. Did you guys try a new carburetor or something?"

Rachel crossed her arms and tilted her head accusingly at Hugo. Back at team headquarters earlier in the week, Meline had suggested changing the fuel intake manifold and her uncle, against her recommendation, had given Meline the go-ahead. Now that they were at the track, there wasn't much they could do. The only positive outcome of that decision, from her standpoint, had been finally getting Hugo's concession for her to make at least a few minor tweaks in the exhaust system of the backup motor.

Either her uncle was giving Meline all the rope he needed to hang himself, or he didn't trust Rachel. Maybe both.

"Bring her in, Justin," Hugo said.

Rachel threw her clipboard down on top of a tool cabinet and paced in the shadows. Wade and Hugo discussed the situation while they waited for the No. 448 car to make it back to the garage. Within minutes, the deep and loud roll of a stock car rumbled to a stop outside the Fulcrum garage and Justin hopped out. "I can't race tomorrow with that engine!"

"What do you suggest we do?" Hugo asked.

Rachel gritted her teeth. She couldn't fault Hugo for gathering all possible information before making a decision, but knowing it was the right thing to do made it no less frustrating.

"Hell, I don't know." Justin yanked off his gloves. "Change the damned engine."

"This isn't qualifying," Wade reminded them. "We've already been through inspections. We put in a new engine and you start at the back of the pack for the race tomorrow."

"I don't care. I had a crappy qualifying time anyway. Won't make much of a difference moving to the back. Just give me some power, so I can move up fast."

"Rachel?" Hugo called for her.

She stopped pacing and glanced at her uncle.

"Did you finish with those adjustments you wanted to make on the exhaust manifold of the backup motor?"

She nodded, her heart suddenly racing faster than the No. 448 car. If they used the engine she'd changed and Justin finished poorly, she'd go back to Fulcrum Monday morning with her tail between her legs. If he finished well… She smiled.

"Did you have time to test it?"

"Yes, sir. Four hours on the dyno."

"And?"

"The stats were better than that engine you got right now."

Hugo looked at Wade. "Change it."

Rachel could hardly breathe. This was it. Showtime.

DAMN, THOSE GUYS ARE moving fast.

In a stream of colors and a roar of sound, the cars sped by Payton, one after another, at the race track outside of Charlotte. Payton would rather sit out a blizzard on Mount Hunter than go one lap around that track with forty-three cars zooming by at 180 miles an hour.

It was another Saturday night, and this race was the longest of the season. Payton looked at the time. Talk about stamina. Those drivers had been on that track for close to five long, hot hours. He didn't care what anyone said, this was the one that had started it all, the original extreme sport.

He finally had to admit it. Sometime during the past several weeks Payton had developed a great deal of respect for these NASCAR guys. Each one of the drivers, fearless, strong and intensely competitive, got out there every week and faced their fears. Maybe if Payton got the contract with NSN he could still do one or two NASCAR shows a year and keep in touch with these guys.

Only it wasn't just the drivers. He had come to respect the teams as a whole. The strategies, the fast pace, the endless hours. Talk about commitment. They didn't plan one race a year as he had for his climbing expeditions. These folks had to be on top of their game all but two months out of the year.

He'd climb with any one of them, especially Rachel. That woman took her job more seriously than most climbers he'd met. If he couldn't talk her into climbing with him, maybe her brother would go. Payton would love to get that guy on the end of a rope.

Today, though, Justin was having a tough race. Before the race had started, he'd heard a rumor about Fulcrum changing the engine in the No. 448 car. He'd gone straight to Rachel's garage to make sure everything was okay. She'd told him they were trying out some of her changes on the exhaust system. She'd been stressed but excited. This was a big race for her.

Amazingly, the No. 448 car had managed to move from last place at the beginning of the race up to tenth, but one problem after another had kept Justin from moving into first. Either he'd been too tight, or too loose. Now, around lap 380 and closing in on the end of the race, he was falling back.

Come on, Justin, stay with it. Payton watched the nearest TV monitor, but he'd had his headset tuned to exclusively the No. 448 car's frequency for most of the race, despite strict instructions from the station manager to cover all drivers equally.

Someone tapped Payton's shoulder, dragging his concentration away from the race. He turned to find Neil behind him with his camera on his shoulder. "Are we filming or what?" Neil asked.

"Did you get some footage of Kent Grosso's car?"

Some crazy animal rights activists, protesting Kent's sponsor, Vittle Farms, had managed to throw paint all over the No. 427 car. Unfortunately, it'd happened after qualifying and inspections, so Kent Grosso, forced to use his second car, had been thrown into the back of the pack along with Justin for the start of today's race.

"Yeah, I got it," Neil said.

"How 'bout some action clips from the Maximus pit?"

"Good idea. Where are you going?"

"Back to Fulcrum."

"Figures." Neil took off for Kent Grosso's pit area.

Payton headed toward the No. 448 car's pit and stopped several feet shy of the action, hoping he wouldn't distract Rachel. Hat and headset on, she sat atop the war wagon with Hugo and Wade, watching the race on several monitors. She seemed intense, but composed.

As if sensing his presence, she glanced down and searched the small crowd gathered around their pit area. On spotting him, she mouthed, "Thanks for coming."

He tipped his hand and nodded. He would've loved being up there with her right now overseeing things, supporting her and the team and talking with Justin. There was certain to be more discussion going on between Hugo, Rachel and Wade than what was coming over Justin's radio frequency. Maybe even some yelling as they'd been trying for the last several hours to figure out how to get the best possible performance out of the No. 448 car.

As if to prove his point, Rachel leaned over to Hugo, pointed at their monitor and said something off radio. Payton glanced at the monitor nearest him for a quick snapshot of the race standings and to see if he could figure out what Rachel was worried about.

Over the radio, he heard Hugo say to Justin, "What's going on?"

"My tires won't last," Justin said, an edge to his normally calm voice. Payton could hear his frustration building. "This track is rough today. And hot."

"Thirty to go," Dennis Murphy, Justin's spotter, said, referring to the number of laps left in the race.

"Stay loose." Hugo's calm voice came through the headset. "We might get lucky with a caution."

Justin released a puff of frustration. "Rachel, I can't get what I need out of this car."

Sounding more annoyed than her brother, she said, "I hear you." She sat back, crossing her arms and glancing back down at Payton, her brow furrowed with concern.

Payton put his hands up by his face and crossed his fingers. Though he certainly knew more about cars and stock racing than he did a few months ago and wanted to reassure Rachel that everything was going to be okay, the truth was he didn't know Jack about the problems they were experiencing today.

Rachel turned back to her own monitor. "We need a bite change," she said. "He should come in."

"It's a green flag," Wade cautioned.

"My tires aren't gonna last, anyway," Justin countered.

"Come on in then," Hugo gave the order to pit. "Whaddya want done, Rachel?" Payton could hear the infinite patience in Hugo's voice. Whether she knew it or not, her uncle was training her, maybe even to take his place someday.

"A round of wedge from the right rear," she said quickly, giving the pit crew orders.

"Wade?"

"Sounds good," Wade said. "Let's give it a shot."

Payton marveled at the symmetry of Fulcrum's pit crew at work. The men flew over the wall and worked together at lightning speed. A quick zip in and out and the No. 448 car was back on the track.

"How's it feel now?"

"Too loose," Justin said.

"So be it," Hugo said. "Focus on finishing this race."

"But, Hugo—" Rachel sounded frustrated.

"Gotta let some things ride, Rachel," Hugo said. "Everything can't be perfect on a race track."

Rachel looked back down at Payton and frowned. Payton shrugged and mouthed, "He's right." She clenched her jaw and looked away. Justin ran a few more laps and managed to hold his position.

Someone tapped Payton's shoulder again. It was Neil.

"Did you get some action from Kent Grosso's pit?" Payton asked.

"Yep, and a couple other drivers, too."

"Great. Thank you." Payton kept one eye on the screen to continue monitoring the race.

"Payton," Neil said, sounding exasperated. "Justin Murphy isn't the only driver on that track."

"I know. Gimme a couple more minutes. The race is almost over." A caution flag came out due to another car blowing a tire, and Payton flipped his headset back in place to listen.

"Come on in," Hugo said. "Rachel, what's next?"

"Adjust the tire pressure," Rachel said.

"Will do."

The No. 448 got back on the track and the caution was raised. "She's still loose, but not bad." Justin sounded excited for the first time in more than an hour. Over the course of the next ten or so laps, the No. 448 car moved ahead—into second place.

"Eleven to go," Dennis reported on the laps remaining.

"You got a three-wide behind you," Hugo said. "One of 'ems gonna make a move."

"I got him," Justin said.

"The No. 427 car's chomping at the bit to get by that threesome."

Kent Grosso was on the outside, pushing, threatening to make a move as soon as one of the three cars fell back.

"Crash! Behind you," Dennis said. "You're clear."

A car on the inside of the three-wide spun out and sent the driver next to him into the wall, and then all the way across the track and into the infield, spewing a cloud of smoke along the way. The drivers were okay, but some of them wouldn't finish today's race.

Justin yelled over the radio, "I'm in trouble!"

"What's happening?" Rachel asked. Payton quickly glanced up at her. She was glued to the monitor, her knees bouncing with nerves.

"I'm tightening up again."

Kent Grosso emerged out of the cloud of smoke too close on Justin's tail.

"Grosso's right on ya."

Feeling completely helpless, Payton could only stand by and watch as Kent smashed into the No. 448 car's rear end, spun down the bank, rolled and came to a stop in the infield. The impact sent Justin whirling toward the infield.

"Dammit!" Payton said aloud.

As the No. 448 car settled in the grass, clouds of dust and chunks of earth flew into the air and Rachel's knee stopped bouncing. "You okay?" she asked Justin, sitting forward and resting her elbows on the tabletop.

"Yeah!" he yelled back, spinning his tires in the dirt, but finally managing to get back out on the track. "Is Kent okay?"

"He's fine," Hugo said. "Stop in here, and let's fix that bumper."

Rachel's gaze connected with Payton's. "He'll finish." He tried to reassure her.

After a quick on and off, the No. 448 was back on the track and making up for lost time. A few more laps and Justin finished fifth. Respectable, yet disappointing after moving all the way from the back of the pack into second. He might've won. On the changes Rachel had made to the engine.

"Hey." Neil tapped Payton's shoulder. "We gotta head to Victory Lane."

"Yeah, I know," Payton agreed. Justin and Kent spinning out left the track open for Bart Branch to take first place by the skin of his teeth. Payton's producer would, no doubt, want an interview with Branch for tonight's local news.

As Payton followed Neil, he passed by the war wagon, reached up for Rachel's hand. She yanked off her headset and looked down at him.

"It's okay," he said, squeezing her fingers. "Justin's okay."

"I know."

"Payton!" Neil yelled. "I'm not filming this alone."

"Go," Rachel said. "I'll be okay."

Strange. Payton couldn't care less about Victory Lane or Bart Branch. All he wanted to do was stay with the Fulcrum team, with Rachel.

CHAPTER NINE

ON HER HANDS AND KNEES, Rachel scrubbed harder and harder to get the last of the construction dirt and grime off her main bathroom floor. If she could only scrub the Charlotte race out of her head, she'd be fine. She couldn't believe all the problems they'd had with the car. Finally, her chance to prove she was right and everything else went wrong.

"Rachel?" A man called her name from the direction of her open front door. The screen door was latched, but it was late, pitch-black outside, making it somewhat unnerving that someone would come down her deserted road.

"Rachel, you home?"

She peeked around the corner and breathed a sigh of relief. Harlan Strom stood behind the screen. "Harlan, what in the world are you doing here this time of night? Don't you ever quit working?" She unlocked the door.

"Oh, I been done working a few hours now." He stepped inside, kept one hand behind his back and avoided her eyes. "I needed to leave your house early to get to another job site, so I didn't have the chance to give these to you when you came home."

He held out several, four or five, old and battered leather-bound books. "One of the guys found these under the floorboards in one of the upstairs bedrooms today."

She took them, ran her hands over the dusty cover of the top book and a tremor shuddered through her. Her parents had built this house, so no one else except her family had lived here. These had to have belonged to one of them.

"They seemed too...personal to leave on the counter."

"Thank you."

"I opened one of 'em. You know, not thinking. I'm sorry." He swallowed. "Looks like they mighta been your mother's."

Rachel asked quite suddenly something she'd never had the nerve to ask anyone before, not even Hugo. Especially not Hugo. "Do you remember her?"

"Sure I do." He nodded, then shook his head. "She sure was pretty. Long red hair. Like yours. You favor your daddy, but every once in a while, when you smile, I see something in your eyes, maybe the color, or the way they crinkle up, that reminds me of her." He fidgeted on his feet. "She wasn't always sad, you know."

"No, I didn't know. I'd always thought for someone to, you know, do what she did, they'd have to be..."

"Oh, naw." He shook his head, dismissing that notion. "She was happy, at least the times I saw her. Had the prettiest laugh, the kind that made you turn around and want to see what sweet thing could possibly have made that sound." He chuckled. "In fact, Hugo and I were with your daddy the night they met. I think it was her laugh that caught Troy's attention."

Rachel smiled, feeling a slight relief in the yawning hunger for a sense of her mother. "Really?"

"She was with some girlfriends at a bar in Rockingham. What was the name of that place? Willy's? Angie's? Ah, hell, I can't remember. But I do recall, it was a Saturday night, and they'd been racing at the old track that day. Back then, sometimes I went with 'em, hung around. Partied."

He shook his head and laughed. "Your daddy told the funniest jokes. He was full of 'em, could go on all night." Then he turned serious. "But don't believe everything you hear, Rachel. No matter what he did or didn't do, he loved your mama. I never saw him look at a woman the way he looked at Ginny. Swept her right off her feet. Ha. Now that I think about it, they were probably married in six months."

He glanced around. "You knew he built this place for her right after they were married, didn't you?"

She nodded.

"She was so happy then, loved the lake."

"I do remember that. I remember her sitting on the dock, dangling her feet in the water. She used to swing me in front of her and dip my toes in, teasing me."

"That sounds like her."

"Do you know…" Rachel blinked back the threatening tears. Anger mixed with uncertainty. No one in her family ever talked about it. "Do you know how she did it?"

Harlan looked confused.

"How did she kill herself, Harlan?"

His expression turned to one of concern. "Why do you want to know this stuff?"

"I *need* to know." She could never ask her uncle and it seemed that missing a few small pieces of this puzzle, somehow, left big gaps in her soul.

"She swallowed a bottle of sleeping pills."

Why? she wanted to ask. Why would a young mother take her own life, leave her babies all alone? How could a woman claim to love her children and still choose to leave them?

As if he could read her mind, Harlan added, "No one knows why, Rachel. She didn't leave a note. And none of the wives had a clue there was anything wrong. Troy didn't know what to do, how to handle it, when she got sad. Men...don't... My generation...we don't know how to talk about things, 'specially women things."

"You're doing a great job."

"It'd warm her heart to know you're living here."

"I think so, too." She gave him a hug.

Uncomfortable now, he stepped back and nodded at the books. "I hope it was the right thing. Giving them to you."

"It's the only thing."

"Well, I'll see you later." He opened the screen door and headed down the porch.

"Thank you, Harlan."

After he'd gone, Rachel set the diaries on the vanity in the bathroom and went back to cleaning the floor. She couldn't get her mind off the books and what she might find inside. The covers were dusty and the spines broken from use. Her mother must have written quite a lot.

A niggling voice whispered in the back of her mind. *Read them.* Rachel snatched the books, ran upstairs and, without cracking a cover, closed them in the bottom drawer of her nightstand. She ran her fingers in circles over the flat surface of the skipping stone she'd found a while back down by the lake.

Someday, maybe she'd be ready to read the books.

"BEND YOUR KNEES." Payton studied Rachel's form. "That forces you to use only your arms. You won't be able to use your legs to lift the weights."

"I'm doing bicep curls. How could I possibly use my legs to lift weights that are in my hands?"

"Try it. See if you can feel the difference."

She did and laughed. "They feel heavier. I should've known that would happen, but it's still amazing."

She was amazing. And strong. And beautiful. He watched her muscles bunch and release.

When she'd come out of the Fulcrum headquarters' locker room a half hour earlier in a white tank top and black shorts, he'd lost all interest in working out. Her body was a precise balance of curves and muscles that he already knew fit perfectly in his arms. He had a feeling she'd fit better under him, or smack-dab on top of him. He hadn't been able to get that comment she'd made the other night about the possibility of them sleeping together out of his mind.

Good thing they weren't alone.

Though it was the Monday afternoon after the Charlotte race, several guys from another Fulcrum team, Shakey Paulson's crew, were doing circuits on the weights and two women were using the ellipticals. Fulcrum's gym was fairly well-equipped with a variety of aerobic equipment and a full range of weight-lifting machines. TVs had been mounted in strategic viewing positions and several choice walls, including the free weights area, had been covered with floor-to-ceiling mirrors.

"What do you usually do when you work out?" she asked.

"Weights most of the time. Throw in a couple days a week of aerobic stuff." He lay back on a bench and did some presses, keeping the weights light so he wouldn't need a spotter. "Except for when I have to travel to the races. I run into problems there." After three sets of fifteen, he sat up. She was doing bent-over rows, her bottom kicked out, and he was once again reminded of her perfect form.

He had to refocus. His two-week deadline for getting a Rachel interview was up as far as Jay Wilson was concerned. Payton would likely be able to avoid his boss for another week or so, buying some extra time but, after that, Jay would likely pull Payton completely off the Rachel trail. Payton couldn't let that happen. "Do you think I could come in here and do some filming?"

She frowned. "In the gym?"

"I was thinking in your garages, or offices." He'd only caught a glimpse of the main facility, but it looked perfect for what he had in mind. "Catch you and Hugo and Justin working. You know, in-your-element kind of stuff."

She didn't say anything.

"That way you'd be on your own turf. For the interview." He had to give it a shot.

She smiled at him in the mirror. "We're back to that again, huh?"

"Well, since you won't sleep with me…yet."

She laughed.

"I promise. I won't put anything on the final cut you don't want."

"I'll think about it." She put her head down.

"So what did they decide about your engine adjustments yesterday?" he asked, surprising himself by being genuinely interested in her answer.

She dropped the weights and her mouth opened like a floodgate. "Justin drove an almost perfect race. Moved up from last place. Well, you saw it. He might've won if we'd had the right shocks…."

She went on to describe in detail the problems they'd had figuring out the suspension issues in dealing with another night race. He partially understood the part about how it hadn't been as hot as they'd expected, so as it cooled down even more, the car setup had been tricky. Most of it went right over his head. In either case, he loved watching her face when she talked about something she cared about. He got to see the race all over again through her eyes.

"There was so much going on at the Charlotte race, it's hard to put all the pieces together. I still don't know what happened with the tires right before Kent Grosso hit Justin. I have to examine the data." She wrapped it up with a heavy sigh. "Thanks for coming to the pit, Payton. Having you there helped me stay focused."

Friends. He smiled inside. "What did Meline do when he found out Hugo switched out the engines?"

"Off the record, right?"

"Off the record."

"Blamed the suspension problems on me overcompensating for the cooling track."

The warm-fuzzy feelings disappeared. "You're kidding?"

"Par for the course." She shrugged. "He's taking apart the first engine now to figure out what went wrong." She grabbed the weights again and pumped them furiously. All of a sudden she stopped and turned to him, sweat beading on her brow.

"What?" he asked.

"Take me climbing."

Excited, he dropped the bar. The prospect of teaching her to climb, of sharing with Rachel something that had been so important in his life for so long thrilled him. "Are you serious?"

"Totally."

"Why?"

"I don't know." Her gaze was serious, her eyes piercing. "It feels like something I have to do."

That he could understand. "When do you have a day off?"

"Next Monday. After Dover."

"You're on."

CHAPTER TEN

"DON'T LOOK DOWN," Payton said.

Of course, that's the first thing Rachel did. Twenty feet of open air was all that stood between her and where Payton sat on a rock. Then again, twenty feet was nothing. The dizzying part was hanging from a sheer cliff on the east face of Crowders Mountain on a section called David's Castle, eight-hundred-some-odd feet above the surrounding relative flatland of Gaston County.

With her hands above her head, fingers gripping practically nonexistent handholds and her feet twisted sideways, barely balancing on narrow ledges, she couldn't focus. The countryside blurred into a mass of blue and green, green and blue. The gray-and-pink rock smelled hot, and she was sweating with fear. As if it wasn't already beating fast enough, her heart took off as if it were charging to the finish line on any given Sunday.

"I can't do this," she said, clenching the rock tighter.

"Yes, you can."

"No. I can't."

"Relax, Rachel," Payton said, his resonant voice soft and encouraging. "You're not going anywhere. I've got you."

She was wearing a harness, which was tied to the end of the rope. The rope, in turn, was cinched through a figure-eight metal contraption that Payton said would take most of her weight if she fell. All of it, the weight distribution, the angles, the connections, made complete sense from an analytical standpoint, but, in reality, if he happened to let go of the rope, she was dead.

He'd called it belaying. She called it crazy.

"I suppose this is a bad time to tell you I'm afraid of heights."

"Rachel, honey, you can do this," he said, not buying her comment for a second. "I know it."

The only thing she knew at the moment was that if she clutched the rock any harder, her fingers might fall off from lack of blood. "Promise you won't drop me?" She held herself as close to the rock face as the knot attaching her to the rope allowed.

"I promise." His soft, rumbling chuckle did something funny to her stomach, distracting her for a second. "Let go of the rock face and sit back on the rope."

"You *are* crazy!"

"Hang there. Feel it."

"And if the rope breaks?"

"That won't happen. It's tested for thousands of pounds. Remember? And you watched how I connected the climb topside. Do you remember that bolt I hooked the rope through? That ain't coming loose."

And because she'd insisted, he anchored the rope again, to a huge boulder with some webbing, straps of brightly colored, tightly woven material. He'd shown her how all the knots were tied and how they wouldn't come loose no matter how hard he yanked and pulled and stretched. He explained the strength of all the equipment, that the carabiners and cables were made of high-test metal. In fact, he'd explained every movement he made every step of the way.

Then he'd tossed the two ends of the rope to the ground, what seemed one-hundred-plus feet below them, and they'd hiked down to the bottom of the climb. He'd tied one end of the rope to her seat harness and kept the other one for himself. He explained that as she climbed up, he'd take in the slack. If she did lose her grip and fall, she'd never drop more than a few feet. It seemed like an awful lot of work to put yourself through this agony.

"You keep clenching the rock and your forearms are gonna burn and then crash," he said. "Give yourself a rest. Lean back."

"I suck at this." She panted. Her breath hit the cool rock and bounced back into her eyes.

"Everyone has moments of panic, especially when you're starting out. Once you get a feel for it, you'll be climbing five tens in no time."

She swallowed and rested her cheek against the cool rock. Another minute and her arms would fail.

"Sweetheart, take a deep breath and sit back."

The endearment took the heat right out of her fear. She even heard a bit of North Carolina charm sneak into his California accent. "How do I do that?"

"Simple. Let go. Use your feet to keep from banging against the rocks. Flatten your climbing shoes against the rock face and bend your knees. That harness wrapped around your butt will act like a chair."

She tried to imagine herself letting go. "I can't do it."

"Rachel, would I let you get hurt?"

"No."

"Then trust me."

Amazingly, she did trust Payton. Probably more than she'd ever trusted any man outside of her brother and uncle. Without giving herself another second to think about it, she held her breath and let go. The rope stretched somewhat, but held. *I did it.* She smiled, feeling a little like Spider-Woman.

"Bounce around. Get comfortable."

"I don't think so."

"It feels good. Try it."

She bent her knees, pushed off from the rock and bounced in and out. She looked down at Payton. "This *is* fun."

"Told ya." He was grinning, his dark sunglasses hiding his eyes.

"Okay, so you won't drop me and the rope won't break. Now what?"

"Climb to the top, and then I'll belay you down."

That didn't sound so hard. Maybe she *could* do this. She reached for a big knob on the rock face, drew herself in and fumbled for another handhold, found placement for her feet and stood.

Payton had bought her a pair of climbing shoes that squished her toes together like sardines in a can. "You have to get your weight over the rock," he'd explained about the tight fit. The soles and sides of the shoes were covered in sticky rubber that gripped the rough rock surface.

"One hold after another," he said. "Before you know it, you'll be at the top."

She made several moves, went higher. "I don't see where to go?"

"There's a ledge by your left foot." She moved her foot around, searching for the hold. "Your *left,*" he said as her foot floundered for purchase. "Your other left."

She chuckled, realizing she'd been searching for the ledge with her right. "Very funny."

"There you go. Once you feel it, put all your weight on your left foot and stand."

She did exactly what he'd said and climbed several feet.

"I had a feeling you'd be good at this. Your balance is incredible."

Energized, she went higher and higher. This was amazing. With every movement, an uncanny connection with her body grew stronger. Until the muscles in her arms burned. "It's getting harder."

"You're at a slight overhang. Requires more arm strength. A few more feet and it'll get easier. Don't give in. You're almost to the top."

He was dead-on. Several more moves and she was able to flatten her body against the rock, balance on her feet and let her arms drop to her sides for a rest. She stretched her screaming muscles. "How could you have done this for hours at a time?"

"I always climbed with a partner. You lead for a while, and while you're belaying your partner, your muscles rebound."

Ten more feet. Another overhang, and that was it.

"When you're ready, go for it, Rach."

She reached overhead and found her pace again. Within minutes, her fingers curled solidly over a ninety-degree angle of rock. She'd made the top. "How do I get up and over this ledge?"

"You've got to feel this one on your own. And I have to give you some slack, otherwise you won't be able to get yourself over the top. Okay?"

"Okay." She felt his hold on the rope loosen and a

momentary sense of panic followed. There was nothing to hold. Nothing she could use to lever herself over the top. And this time if she fell there was slack in the rope.

"Use your legs."

That did it. She inched upward, managed to get her elbows onto the top ledge and transfer her weight. She threw her foot over the top, pushed on her knee. "I did it!" she yelled.

"You sure did." He laughed.

"I can't believe it." She looked down the one hundred or so feet at him and grinned. "That was awesome." She felt strong, powerful, an I-am-woman-hear-me-roar sense of accomplishment coursed through her.

Payton held a hand over his eyes. "How's it feel up there?"

"Like I'm on the top of the world." She couldn't imagine what he must have felt reaching the summit of his climbs, places where he truly had been at the top of the world. This feeling, this adrenaline high, could be addictive.

Pointing eastward, toward a town with a baby-blue water tower, she practically yelled, "I can see Gastonia right over— Oh, my! I can see Charlotte!" The city sky-scrapers, manmade stalagmites, shot out from the relatively flat ground. "Clear as a bell. It's as if I can see the entire state of North Carolina. Lakes and trees. The sky. So blue. Is that Lake Norman?" There she went running off at the mouth again.

"Amazing, isn't it?"

She wished Payton were by her side. He wasn't smiling anymore. "What's the matter?"

"Nothing." He shook his head. "You look pretty cool up there."

"Now what?"

"Sit back over the edge and let me belay you down."

"What?"

"Sit back. I'll lower you down."

Eighty feet down. Another hurdle.

"Did you have to do this on the mountains you climbed?" As soon as the question left her mouth, she realized how silly it sounded.

"I had no other way down my climbs, Rachel. You can untie yourself and walk down here if you want."

Strangely enough, she didn't want to walk down. That might taint this perfect day.

"You can do it," he encouraged her. "I gotcha."

She went to the edge, turned around, gripped the rope and let herself fall back. He dropped her down. She used her feet to keep from crashing into the rock. "Woohoo!" There was something so freeing about swaying through the air. Better yet, there was something so empowering about making that climb.

"Put your feet down," he yelled. "Or you're gonna hit the ground. Watch out."

She pushed away from the wall one last time and let her feet come softly to the ground. "That was amazing." She reached down to the rope and tried undoing the knot. Her arms were shaking, the muscles suddenly mush.

"Off belay." Grinning, Payton unhooked himself from the figure eight and stood. "Let me take care of that. Your arms are probably shot." He grabbed the knot to work it free. The motion tugged her closer. Close enough to smell the sunshine in his hair.

"Thank you," she whispered.

The knot was temporarily forgotten. "I knew you could do it."

"I didn't." She was hot and sweaty, her arms felt as if they might fall off from her shoulders and all she could think to do was kiss him.

His gaze traveled to her lips and back to her eyes. "Now it's my turn." He quickly undid the knot.

"Turn for what?"

He took the end of the rope, looped it through his own harness, and tied a complicated knot.

"Me? Belay you? No, no, no. You've got to be close to two hundred pounds."

"One hundred and eighty-five. And my weight doesn't matter." He steered her toward the flat rock he'd been sitting on and hooked a carabiner attached to that metal belaying contraption onto her harness. After putting the rope into her hands, he showed her how to belay. "If I fall, jerk the rope down and you could hold me up there all day if you had to."

"This isn't a good idea."

"You can do this, too."

"Payton—"

"One hand. On the rope. At all times." He walked to the base of the climb. "On belay." He started up the rock face. He swiftly climbed five feet and stopped. "I'm gonna sit back so you can see what it feels like."

"Wait! Wait!" She sat down and went through the steps. Left hand pulled the slack in. Right hand took through the figure eight. Hand on the rope at all times.

Left hand. Right hand. One hand on the rope all the time.

"Ready?"

"As ready as I'll ever be."

"Here I go."

The rope stretched taut with his weight, but she held him. Effortlessly. He was right. There she was holding him suspended in the air four feet off the ground as if he weighed no more than a newborn. The figure eight created so much friction his weight was nothing.

"Pretty cool, isn't it?"

"I can't believe it."

"Here I go again." He swung himself toward the rock and started climbing. "This is where you take in the slack," he said. "Make sense?"

"I got it."

Left hand. Right hand. One hand on the rope all the time.

As she pulled in the slack in the rope, she watched him climb in fluid, coordinated motions. Hand, hand, foot, foot. In only a minute or two, he'd scaled the rock face and was near the top. "I'm gonna fall back again."

"No, no, no!"

"Ready."

"Payton."

"Here I go."

"Ah!" she screamed and gripped the rope.

He hung, suspended in the air, swinging back and forth and laughing.

"What if you'd fallen?"

"I couldn't fall. *You* got me."

"You are so crazy. Get down from there right now."

"You want me down, you have to do it yourself."

"Ha! Maybe I'll let you swing there all day long."

"I'm all yours."

"Smart aleck." She reversed the belaying process, letting rope feed back through the figure eight, slowly, until his feet touched the ground.

"I can't believe you did that." She unhooked her harness and stood. More afraid of dropping him than of falling herself, adrenaline hit her hard.

He untied the knot and walked over to her. "I trust you."

"You're an idiot."

"Am not." He took hold of her shoulders, bent his head and kissed her. Kissed her.

He felt and tasted so good, hard muscle and wet warmth. She leaned into him, opened her mouth and wrapped her arms around his neck. He picked her up, set her on a rock ledge and stepped into her. The smooth rock face was cool against her back and she found herself inching closer and closer toward Payton's warmth.

He inched away for a moment. "Thanks for giving me a reason to get out here." Resting his forehead against hers, he smiled into her eyes. "That's the first time I've climbed since my fall."

She sucked in a breath. "Weren't you scared?"

"Maybe a little. But I knew you had me." He gave her another quick kiss. "Wanna go again? I hear there's a climb around here called Four Play."

"Do you ever stop?"

"Never. I stop I die."

CHAPTER ELEVEN

HARLAN TOSSED the last load of scrap from Rachel's kitchen into the Dumpster outside. His stomach grumbled. It was getting late, and he should be heading home. Though he wouldn't mind trying, he couldn't avoid Catie forever. He had to sleep sometime.

She'd been as relentless this past week as a nail gun jammed on automatic. "Did you talk to Rachel? Did you? Huh? Huh?" She wouldn't let it go anytime soon. Her sixteenth birthday was approaching and she wanted that car drivable, which meant the engine had to be finished.

The sound of a vehicle came from Rachel's long drive. Someone was coming, but it wasn't Rachel. A Honda pulled into the driveway and Rachel climbed out of the passenger's seat. That sportscaster fella, carrying a bag of groceries, joined her in front of the house. This was something new. What was going on with these two?

"Hey, Rachel."

"Hi, Harlan. How're you doing?"

"Good. We pretty much finished with the kitchen today. Painting's done. Got the light fixtures in…"

"I can't wait to see it."

"And, well…" he said, staring at her. "Everything went

fine." He must look a complete doofus to her. "Not much left to do now."

"Thanks, Harlan. You've done such a great job," Rachel said, staying back with him when the sportscaster headed up to the steps. "Is there anything I can do for you?"

Uneasy, he looked around. Anywhere but at Rachel. "There is something." He couldn't ask her to fix Catie's engine, but maybe... "I've never taken Hugo up on his offers to get me pit passes. Usually worry about getting in the way, but now my daughter, Catie...well...she..."

"I remember Catie. Haven't seen her since she was little." Rachel held out her hand about waist high.

That would've probably been at Lynette's funeral. "Anyway, she's kind of a racing fan. Do you think you could get us track passes?"

"Shoot, Harlan, we just missed the Charlotte and Dover races, and it's probably too late for Pocono. Hmm, I might be able to swing Michigan." Her brow creased in concentration. "Would you like to fly with the Fulcrum team to New Hampshire?"

He thought for a minute and nodded. "I can do that." She probably wouldn't be able to manage anything this late.

"Technically, Catie's too young to get into the field," she said. "But I'll pull a few strings and get some hot passes for you."

"Really?"

"Sure. We'll count you in. And Catie."

Ah, hell. Now he'd done it.

BOOKSHELVES AND an entertainment center had been built into the south wall in the main living area of Rachel's house, but the space was still mostly a jumbled mess of sawhorses and tools, lengths of wood trim and molding. "They still have to paint and carpet in here," Rachel said on her way through the room.

In her kitchen, granite countertops of mottled blacks and browns together with gold flecks had been installed, as well as a sink and a wide slat wooden floor. The walls had been painted a pale olive-green and everything contrasted perfectly with the white cabinets. A new table and chairs had been delivered and sat, still packed in plastic and protective cardboard, pushed out of the way. What appeared to be a large area rug was rolled into a big tube and stood in the corner.

"Harlan wasn't kidding," Payton said, glancing around. "Your kitchen's finished."

Rachel's shoulders rose on a heavy sigh. "They get a lot done while I'm out of town. Problem is that when I'm here, I haven't time to clean and arrange everything." She'd taken her one and only day off during the week to go climbing with him.

"Then let's do it," he said. "Put your kitchen together."

"Now?"

"Why not?" He set the bag of groceries on the countertop. "I can wait to eat."

Her face lit with excitement. "You put the groceries away and I'll get the vacuum."

Forty-five minutes later, they stood back and admired the results. Everything sparkled, from the countertops to the refrigerator to the beveled-glass cabinet inserts, and it all went together without appearing overly manipulated.

He steered her over by the center island and stepped

back. She'd chosen her colors well. "You fit in your kitchen."

"Shut up." She laughed. "Let's eat."

They grilled burgers and cut fresh fruit and ate on the new furniture on her backyard deck facing Lake Norman. By the time they'd finished, it was late. Payton was all set to head home when Rachel said, "Let's go down to the water."

"I got the feeling that area was strictly off-limits."

"It was."

"Was?"

"Now it's not."

He didn't want to think too hard about what that meant or didn't mean. No commitments or expectations was fine by him.

They walked down to the water's edge. It was pitch-black outside, but for the sliver of a moon reflecting off the lake and a few lights dotting the opposite shoreline. Crickets chirped from the nearby woods and an owl hooted from some distant perch.

Payton searched through some rocks, before finding one he liked and skipping it across the surface of the water. "What is it about a calm lake? Makes me want to cause ripples."

"Me, too." She laughed.

They each skipped a few more rocks and then, by unspoken agreement, sat down in the swing. Payton stretched out, his arms along the back side. Rachel curled her feet under her and seemed content to let him rock them both back and forth.

"Do you remember your parents?" he asked. He knew it was a heavy topic, but he wanted to know. Good, bad or indifferent, he wanted to know everything about Rachel.

"My dad barely at all. I don't remember liking him, or not liking him. From what Hugo and other people say, he probably wasn't around much." She tilted her face to the sky. "I think he must have had rough skin."

"Why?"

"Every time I shake someone's hands that are rough, I have an instantaneous thought of my dad. Not a face. I don't remember what he looked like. It's more as if I'm infused with…not really a memory…more of an aura for a split second. Then it's gone. I guess it makes sense with him working on cars all the time."

"What about your mom?"

"Mama? I have a whole jumble of…I'm not really sure if they're hazy memories or…dreams of her. Like whenever I smell fried chicken, or hear it sizzling in a frying pan, this image comes to me. I'm sitting on a hard, cool floor, maybe the kitchen, and I must be really little, because I'm crawling inside a cabinet. It feels dark and safe. I can hear her voice, at least I think it's her voice, saying, 'Where's Rachel?' It always makes me happy." She smiled. "Could've been a dream, though."

"You could've been playing hide-and-seek and were excited she couldn't find you."

"Maybe. I'm not really sure." She leaned back. "I can't believe I'm telling you this."

"Why?"

"Reporter."

"Friend. First." He'd told her so much about himself, and suddenly, that surprised him. He nestled her into the crook of his arm. "Tell me more about your mom."

"That's the only happy memory I have." She snuggled against him and sighed. "The rest… When I think of

Mama, I get sad. I think she was sad. Soft and warm, but sad. Honestly though, I'm never sure if these things really happened, or if they're some kind of remnant of a dream. You know?"

He nodded.

"I think I made her cry once," she said, surprised the words had come from her mouth.

"You were little. It couldn't have been your fault."

"I think maybe it was. We were down here by the lake. I remember feeling hot and sandy. And tired. Probably, she wanted to take me into the house for a nap. I suppose I threw some kind of tantrum. The terrible twos and all that. I think she started crying. The next thing I remember is waking up hungry. We must have both fell asleep on the beach. Right about there." She pointed twenty feet away in the grass.

The night turned silent, the lake seemed to hold its breath. Fireflies lit and disappeared near the surface of the grass.

"I've never told anyone this. Sometimes, I wonder if I made her kill herself. That it was something I did, or didn't do that sent her over the edge."

He looked out over the water. "Understandable, yet impossible for a two-year-old."

"Intellectually, I know that. Emotionally, it's there. Pounded into me, like dents on a fender."

"Feelings aren't logical. Attempting to make sense out of them will only get you into trouble."

"Refusing to acknowledge them doesn't make them go away." She shook her head. "In fact, the more I try to not think about things, the more angry I get. I can't help but feel as if Mama and Daddy left me and Justin. As if they'd had a choice and we'd been abandoned. My mom did choose, though, didn't she?"

"She was sick, Rachel. She didn't know what she was doing."

"Daddy wasn't any better, living that risky lifestyle. A lot of people think someone ran him down on purpose. An angry husband. Another driver he'd wronged in some fashion."

"Why'd you want to live out here with that kind of baggage piled all around?"

She was quiet for a moment. "Some say my daddy bought this place to keep Mama out of town. That way he could cause any kind of trouble and she'd never know about it." Rachel took a deep breath and sighed. "I think it was the only nice thing he ever did for her. She loved being out here, loved the lake. Sunrise down here by the water. Here, I can keep connected to the past without staying there. Does that make sense?"

"No."

"I figured if I could make some new memories, some good ones, that'd help me move past the bad ones."

"Maybe you should have left instead. Clean break. Started over somewhere."

"Like you did? After your daddy died?"

He nodded.

"I couldn't do that."

"How do you know until you give it a shot?"

"I tried in college. Enrolled at RIT in New York. For engineering." She laughed. "Didn't last one single semester. I was so homesick, called home every night and cried myself to sleep on the phone. Virginia Tech was a much better choice. I went home every weekend."

He shook his head. "I haven't been home in six years. Not since my youngest brother got married."

"I'll bet they miss you."

"They've got each other."

"So they get together, but not you?"

"They all live within forty to fifty miles of each other near San Francisco."

"You don't get along with them?"

"We get along fine. I just don't…feel the need to be a part of their lives."

"Huh. I can't imagine that."

"Like I can't imagine living parts of your life. Being so involved with your family. Getting tied down."

"I'm not tied down."

"You'd never leave North Carolina, would you?"

"Never."

"Case closed."

WEDNESDAY MORNING before the Pocono race, Rachel sat at her office desk, her right knee bouncing with nervousness, and watched the tape one more time. If Hugo couldn't convince owner Dixon Rogers to cough up the rental fee for another shot in the wind tunnel to prove her theories about changing the angles of the pipes in the exhaust manifold, let alone more rental time on the chassis simulator, then the tape from the first session would have to do.

She reran it a second, third, fourth time and focused exclusively on how the splitter of the new NASCAR Sprint Cup Series car design affected the air as it hit the front end. That had to be messing with the exhaust flow, more than they'd originally expected. This was aerodynamics, someone else's job, and not her problem. But the engineer, the perfectionist, in her couldn't let it go.

Sitting back in her chair, she noticed her arms ached, and her butt was sore. What the heck? *Climbing*. Crowders Mountain. She'd felt strong, almost invincible.

Dammit. She was sick of taking the heat for these engine problems. Today, Meline was going to listen to her. Heart racing, she pushed off from her desktop and found him in the main assembly room on his cell phone.

"Go ahead and take the patio furniture, but I want the big-screen TV," he said, first glancing at her and then looking away. "Yes, the one in the great room. What do you think?" He paused, holding the phone away from his ear.

The voice on the other end of the line, probably his soon-to-be-ex wife, sounded quite irate.

"You gave me that TV for Christmas last year," he continued. "That makes it mine."

This was probably a terrible time to have this discussion, but now that she'd summoned the nerve, she couldn't back down.

"Go ahead. Talk to an attorney. About a TV. I don't care." He clicked his phone off and jammed it back in his belt clip. "I'm busy, Rachel. I've got an appointment in ten minutes."

Her heart raced. "I need to talk to you."

"Later. I'm running late."

Force of habit made her step back. But then she stopped herself. Something inside her no longer appreciated the feeling of stepping back and away. She tried to remember what it felt like to finish that climb on Crowders Mountain, reenergized herself with the same sense of accomplishment. She'd finished something she hadn't thought she could do and she had the sore muscles to prove it.

She could make Meline listen. Whether he wanted to or not. "No, Johnny. Now. This won't take long."

"What is it?"

"We need to talk about the exhaust—"

"Not that again." He rubbed his eyes.

"Yes. That again." Her palms started sweating. "You've never heard me through completely."

"I don't need to. I already know you're full of it."

She was full of it? Oh, no. She swallowed and calmly formed her argument. "Johnny, you haven't looked at the wind tunnel tapes since we've been having problems. It's time to reassess."

He took a step toward her. "So you reassess. You're the one who's wrong."

Step back. He's not listening.

From the next workstation behind Meline, Fred and Loren stopped what they were doing and glanced her way. They were friends. Her team. She had a responsibility to them.

She shook her head at Meline. "I'm not letting this go until you come back to my office, watch the tape and listen to what I have to say. If you still think I'm wrong, so be it. But you at least need to listen."

He rolled his eyes.

This wasn't doing any good. He wouldn't be objective. There was no point.

His problem. She had to give it a go. She raised her eyebrows at him. "What are you afraid of, Johnny? That I might be right?"

Fred and Loren smiled, gave her a thumbs-up sign.

"Let's get this over with. Once and for all." He stalked off to her office.

"Watch the air when it hits the splitter." She reran the tapes and stood back to let him watch. When the tape finished, she asked, "Did you see it?"

"What exactly do you think I should see?"

They talked briefly about the effect of the airflow on the engine, but Meline was having none of it. "This is aerodynamics," he said. "Not our problem."

"It is if it affects the engine. I think we need to adjust the exhaust manifold."

"We already made changes to the exhaust system base on the new car design."

"Not enough." She crossed her arms to keep her hands from shaking.

"Oh. So because you're a Murphy you think you know everything?"

"What?"

"Don't give me that innocent crap."

"Why are you doing this, Johnny?" Whether it was anger or adrenaline, she wasn't sure, but something made her want to toss her cookies. "Why won't you at least consider the possibility?"

"Because we got it right the first time. Our problems have to do with your adjustments at the track."

"I think you've used that excuse one too many times. Why don't you come to one of the races and prove it?"

"Maybe I will."

CHAPTER TWELVE

"BAD DAY?" Payton asked, almost dropping his cell phone as he took the Mooresville exit off the highway. He hadn't been able to return her call from that afternoon, so he'd decided to bring her some dinner. Well, that and his boss had finally cornered him on the status of an interview with Rachel. He'd convinced Jay to give him one more week.

"Crappy," Rachel said, sounding unusually grumpy.

"What happened?"

"I talked to Meline today."

"You actually confronted him? Good for you."

"Lot of good it did me. He didn't listen."

"Hey, it's a start." He shifted the phone to his other ear. "You sound like you could use some unwinding. What're you doing right now?"

"Some maintenance on my truck."

"That doesn't sound like it's doing the trick."

"It's relaxing. Takes my mind off things."

He laughed. "Motorhead."

"Very funny, coming from a rockhead."

"Touché." Still chuckling, Payton pulled into Rachel's driveway. Her pickup was parked with the hood popped in the middle stall of the three-car garage. All the doors stood wide-open, and even from a distance he could tell the area was clean and orderly, exactly what he'd come to expect from Rachel.

She'd changed from her Fulcrum uniform into jeans and a black T-shirt and was on a step stool, leaning over a front fender of her truck, and probably hadn't heard him driving into her yard. He climbed out of his car, eased the door closed and snuck into her garage.

He marveled at the painted concrete floor, the fact that it was cleaner than most kitchens. A large, clear workbench occupied much of the back wall of the first two stalls. Where there weren't tool cabinets lining the walls, there were shelving units. Lawn and garden supplies and equipment were stored in the stall farthest from the house.

He snuck up beside her, wanted nothing more than to lay his hand on that sexy bottom. This friends business was turning into more of a challenge than he'd thought possible. "Hey, there."

At the sound of his voice, she tilted her head toward him. "Hey, yourself." She snapped her cell phone closed and came out from under the hood. "What are you doing here?"

"Cheering you up." He held out the plastic bag filled with take-out containers. "Brought you dinner. Pork medallions and mashed potatoes from that restaurant in Charlotte."

"That's so sweet." Her brow cleared. "Do you mind waiting to eat until I finish changing the air filter?"

"Not a problem. In fact, I could use an oil change," he said, grinning.

"Very funny. Hand me that wrench on the workbench."

He set their food down. "This wrench?" He held it up.

"That's the one."

He rummaged around in her toolbox. "Sure you wouldn't want a *male* hex, or *female* square? How 'bout a *screw*driver?"

She laughed. "What are you talking about?"

"Haven't you ever noticed how tool names are kinda sexy?"

"Tool names aren't sexy."

"You don't think there's anything suggestive about the term *sensor* or *connector?* Not to mention male and female adaptors."

"Payton." She hopped down from the step stool and reached for his hand. "Give me that wrench."

He held it over her head and managed to back her against the workbench. "Then you got your *chargers,*" he went on, "and your *jacks,*" he said, leaning into her. "Mmm. Ever wonder what a man could do to a woman with a *general service* set?" He put his hands on either side of her, bracketing her against the workbench. He kissed her mouth and moved down her neck.

"You are so bad." She giggled.

"You must have a few favorites. Come on. Tell."

"I've always been partial to the sound of a grinder," she whispered. "Or a bushing. Hammer. Drill." She closed her eyes and groaned. "Is it hot in here?"

He slipped his hand under her T-shirt, ran his palm along her tummy. "Only under these clothes."

"Then maybe we should get them off."

"Oh, man." He looked away. "Don't make suggestions you don't intend to following through on."

"Who says I won't?"

"Me." He was sorry he ever got them heading in this direction. "Let's eat."

"KIM, YOU'VE BEEN VOMITING off and on for more than a week," Rachel said, speaking quietly into her cell phone. A grease rag in her free hand, she was standing inside their garage stall at Pocono, and it was a good thing she was alone. If Hugo and Justin were within earshot, they'd lose it.

"This flu bug's come in handy." In Kim's typically sarcastic manner, she blew the situation off. "My pants were feeling a little tight."

Exasperated, Rachel threw the rag in her hand down onto the rear fender of the No. 448 car. "This is not the flu. You've been losing weight for months."

"So I picked up a parasite from some lettuce in Mexico."

"You haven't been to Mexico!"

"You sure?"

"Stop it. This isn't funny." Rachel paced beside the car, searching for the words to make her cousin see reason.

"Rachel, you worry too much. I'll be fine."

"What have we been telling you? You need to get to a doctor's office. Now. Better yet, the hospital."

"They'll tell me it's a virus and send me home. That's what they always do."

"There's something else going on, Kim. You were complaining of an upset stomach at the race last month. Remember?"

"Morning sickness?"

"You wish." What could she do to get Kim to take this seriously? Beg? Threaten? Both? "Please, promise me you'll go to a doctor."

"Later. Right now I have to get back to work. Those petri dishes can only be neglected for so long."

"Doctor." It was late on Friday afternoon. "Immediately after work. Or I'm coming over there and dragging you to one myself."

"Rachel."

"If you don't promise, I'm telling Justin you're sick again." He'd throw her over his shoulder and carry her if she didn't go on her own.

"Okay, okay. After work. Geesh!"

"Let me know what they say."

"Fine!" Click.

After pulling the wrenches out of her back pocket, Rachel dropped down on a nearby overturned tire and swiped her shoulder across her forehead, doing more to smear the beading sweat than anything. Kim was the closest thing Rachel would ever have to a sister, and she had a feeling she'd completely fall apart if anything happened to her. Kim had always been Rachel's rock.

She pressed the cool metal wrenches against her forehead and tried collecting herself. The team had gone through their practice checklists once already, but, for some reason, Rachel couldn't summon the motivation to run through it all again her ritualistic second and third times. The weather this weekend in Pennsylvania was danged humid, and the forecasters had promised it would get hotter.

She gulped down half a bottle of water and heard the unmistakable sound of Payton's voice bounce around inside the garage. One look at the wrench in her hand and Rachel's thoughts turned to their last conversation. Unbelievably, her skin turned even hotter.

Craning her neck above the tops of the cars, she searched for Payton. Three stalls down, he was interviewing Kent Grosso. Kent's dad, Dean, was leaning against the No. 427 car next to Kent's cousin and spotter, Steve. Disgusted, she tossed the wrench into the nearest toolbox.

Grossos, Grossos. Everywhere you looked. So what else was new?

Over the years, she'd perfected the art of pretending they didn't exist. It was easier on her moods. They were neither here nor there, bad nor good, but it hadn't always been that way. She distinctly remembered the first time she'd noticed Kent. They'd both been around five years old. He was cute and seemed friendly enough, but, even with the innocence of a child, Rachel had known better than to say a word to him.

It wasn't anything her uncle had passed down intentionally or specifically, just something she'd garnered from whispered conversations around the tracks, or the tone of a remark at family gatherings. Grossos were trouble. End of story. She'd never wish track accidents on any one of them but sometimes she wished they'd all drop off the face of the earth.

Strange thing was, Kent had always seemed genuinely nice. So had Sophia, his sister. Even so, what was Justin thinking dating her? Rachel had always known Lucy, his on-again, off-again girlfriend, had never been serious as far as her brother was concerned, but, unfortunately, Sophia was something else entirely. Justin was falling. Big-time. Sometimes, she wanted to shake him silly and point out the obvious in case he'd somehow missed the family memo.

Hello. She's a Grosso.

Just watching Payton talk with them bothered her. As much as he was a NASCAR neophyte, he had to know about the feud between their families. Other than the media, no one ever spoke out loud about it, but it was there all the same as big as Lake Lloyd.

"No problem," Payton was saying. "See you guys later."

Beyond the left rear fender of the No. 448 car Rachel watched all three Grossos head toward the haulers.

"Rachel?" Payton was looking for her.

Knowing she was acting petulant and immature, but probably still feeling vulnerable after her conversation with Kim, she didn't say a word, hunkering farther down.

He came around the back side of the car. "Hey. You okay?"

"I'm fine." She snatched her clipboard from the top of the tool chest and crossed an item off her to-do list.

"You are not fine." He cocked his head at her and lightly tapped between her eyes. "That little furrow right there gives you away."

"What?" She rubbed her forehead.

"Whenever you're angry, you get a furrow of tiny wrinkles between your brows. If it's because you're angry," he said, chuckling, "your eyes are usually flashing. Your jaw might be clenched or your lips flat." He cocked his head in the other direction. "Today you're not mad."

"Yes, I am."

"Today you're upset because your feelings are hurt."

"Is that so?"

"Yep. I can tell by the angle of your eyebrows. Too slanted for angry. Although you're getting there." He opened his arms. "Don't let it sit there. Spit it out. Hit me."

She yanked open a drawer on the toolbox. He was right, dammit, but she couldn't share her concerns about Kim.

That was too much. "Why do you have to interview the Grossos?"

"It's my job."

Petulant and immature, remember? The big question was, was she irritated at the Grossos, worried about Kim or feeling possessive toward Payton? It was a question she didn't want to face.

"Rachel, don't shut me out. I thought we were friends."

Unable to put words to what she was feeling or voice her hurt, she buried her head back under the hood.

He turned away, started to leave the garage. Suddenly, he was bent under the hood, too, right in her face. "You're not being fair."

Now she was angry. "It's not about being fair! It's about feelings."

He backed away, thought for a minute and nodded. "You're right. I've hurt your feelings. I'm sorry."

Amazingly, she felt tears prick the backs of her eyes.

Payton stepped toward her and wrapped his arms around her. "I'm sorry. What do you want me to do?"

She was standing in the infield garage at the Pocono track with a man's arms around her. And it felt good.

"You just did it." She stepped away. "I'll figure my part out."

"Everyone that loves this sport picks their favorite driver, right?" He drew her back, turned her face toward him. "I picked Justin way back. Right after Atlanta."

"Really? You're not saying that to make me feel better?"

He shook his head. "But you can't tell anyone that. I'm supposed to be impartial." Running his thumb over her lips, he said. "Rachel, I may interview the Grossos, the

Branches or any other driver out there, but during a race? I'm with Justin. And you."

That did it. "Still want that interview with me?"

"You know I do."

"You're on." She smiled at him. "Come to Fulcrum headquarters next week."

CHAPTER THIRTEEN

"I CAN'T BELIEVE you talked Rachel into this." Camera in tow, Neil Bukowski followed Payton into Fulcrum Racing's team headquarters.

Payton was excited to see Rachel. He hadn't spoken with her since Pocono last week. He'd had way too much work to do editing his Grosso family special. It was due to air this coming weekend before Michigan.

"I want the camera rolling the whole time," he said, walking into the Fulcrum building. Cold office air hit him full in the face and his voice echoed in the cavernous reception area.

"You're the boss," Neil said.

After the receptionist made a phone call, a PR rep joined Payton and Neil. "Rachel's back in main assembly," he said, shaking their hands. "I'll take you back." He guided them through the heart of the team facilities, the garages. Payton kept him answering mundane questions the whole way. How long has Fulcrum been in these facilities? How many employees? Does the building completely close during December and January, NASCAR's off-season?

The PR rep took them into a huge, warehouse-size garage with identical No. 448 cars lined up in several workstations and a row of Shakey Paulson's cars in others. The first thing that hit Payton was how bright the area was without a single window to the outside world. He wouldn't need any equipment for filming other than a camera. Pale walls and a painted concrete floor reflected the light beaming off rows of fluorescent fixtures dangling from the high ceiling. Bright red tool chests and royal-blue cabinets, along with larger-than-life posters of Justin, Shakey Paulson and owner Dixon Rogers provided a backdrop of color.

This was perfect, most of what he'd need to round out his Murphy show.

They passed several glass-enclosed work areas proving that much of the building was open to public tours. It was tough imagining Rachel working under those conditions, but she probably didn't have a choice. They went through a Staff Only door and found Rachel with several technicians, all of them dressed in Fulcrum garb. She had her arms crossed and was focusing on something one of them was saying.

Her baseball cap, ponytail, Turn-Rite Tools uniform, were the same as when Payton had first met her, but this time when Rachel's gaze caught his, she smiled. For a solid five seconds. Then she spotted Neil and his camera and looked away.

Emotions flashed over her features. Unpleasant memories. Awkward situations. All of a sudden, Payton didn't want to do this to her. He headed toward her, blocking Neil's view and bent his head close. "Maybe this isn't such a good idea."

Her uncertainty cleared. "I've decided this is about showing you, my friend, where I work. What I do. Who

I am." She rubbed his arm, reassuring him. "Besides, you took me rock climbing. A promise is a promise."

"You're sure?"

She nodded. "Are you already taping?"

"The minute we stepped into the reception area," he said, still skeptical.

"Then let's go." She stepped into full camera view, thanked the PR rep and proceeded to give him and Neil a personal tour of the entire facility. They went from the main assembly to fabrication, paint and machine shops, cafeteria, gym, conference rooms and offices. Along the way, Payton noticed that while she was on a first-name basis with every person they passed in the hallways, not everyone was comfortable around her. There were many false smiles and uncertain reactions.

When they got to the personal offices, Payton wasn't surprised to find Rachel's the epitome of cleanliness. There were no half-empty cups of coffee, or odds and ends cluttering her desk. Pencils and pens were neatly arranged in a NASCAR mug, books and manuals were arranged alphabetically on top of her file cabinet and reams of computer printouts were labeled and stacked by date. There wasn't a speck of dust or a coffee ring in sight. Without the framed photo of family angled near her phone, one would have been hard-pressed to determine who occupied this workspace.

"In case it isn't obvious," she said, "I don't spend a lot of time here."

When they got back to the garage bays in the main assembly area, Rachel explained to him, the original NASCAR dummy, "We build the No. 448 cars here, from the bottom up. Frame, chassis, engine block, body. It's all done here." Her eyes lit. "This is where I live."

Payton whispered to Neil, "Fade away, okay?"

"No problem." Neil stepped behind a toolbox and did his best to disappear.

"Let's sit down a minute." Payton directed her toward a stack of tires and had her sit. "I finally get what I need. Some one-on-one Rachel Murphy time."

"In a garage? Probably not what you had in mind." She snickered.

"Hey, you're on camera."

She glanced at Neil. "Final cut, remember?"

"If you cut out anything from my special, I will be very surprised," Payton said. She might be uncomfortable in front of the camera, but she trusted him. Crowders Mountain had made a difference in a lot of ways. He hauled over a chair and started with a few questions he thought might settle her down. "Do you enjoy what you do?"

"Love it."

"Why did you become an engineer?"

She shrugged. "I've always been curious about how things work. Justin and I used to take things apart and race to see who could put them back together the fastest. Hair dryers. Remote-control cars. Radios. Hugo actually encouraged us, even if it meant him having to fix something later. Though he got kind of ticked off when we ruined a TV." She kept her focus on him, her eyes twinkling.

"Who usually won?"

"Me. Justin might be fast on a race track, but put a wrench in my hand and I can run circles around him."

"You should be on the pit crew."

"I'm molasses compared to Loren and Fred and the other guys."

She didn't know it, but she was a natural in front of the camera: her diction was perfect, her voice a charming mixture of sexy and sweet and her smile was bound to touch the most dedicated of the Grosso fans.

"Why do you love racing so much?"

"I love figuring out how to make an engine more efficient, how to make a car go faster. How to create the most power from, basically, a lump of metal and some simple parts."

"Could you see yourself ever doing anything else?"

Her smile disappeared. "Never."

They touched on a lot of things before she began looking tired. Time to wrap it up and move on to some of the other team. "Do you build the engines yourself?"

"No." A nearly imperceptible shadow passed over her features. He should've known that might touch a sore spot. "Johnny Meline's our engine builder. He's over there." She pointed a few bays down to a man talking on his cell phone. "Want to meet him?"

"If it's not too much trouble." He stood and trusted Neil to follow them. Rachel slowed the closer they got to Meline. His tense voice could be heard above the loud garage sounds.

"You never wanted a dog in the first place," he was saying into his cell phone. "No, dammit, I will not pay for the vet bills! Unless they're living with me."

Rachel turned back and whispered, "Divorce."

"No kids, so they're fighting over pets?"

"You got it. Let's find Hugo."

Her uncle was around the other side of the garage bays on his cell phone. "So you're comfortable with this doctor." He paused. "Okay. Let me know." As soon as he saw Rachel, he waved her over. "Love you, too," he said before pocketing the phone. "Kim's waiting on some blood tests."

Rachel nodded. "I talked to her this morning."

"Thanks for convincing her to see someone."

"Took her long enough."

"Payton." Hugo shook his head and smiled. "I didn't figure you for such a slippery son of a gun. Rock climbing in exchange for an interview. Smart move."

"She did good, too."

"That's what I hear. When you stringing me up?" Hugo was probably in his early fifties, but seemed in fairly good shape.

"You serious?" Payton asked.

"Good God, no." Hugo laughed. "Being behind the wheel of one of these stock cars scared me enough. Why in blazes would I want to dangle a hundred feet in the air? Justin'll do it though."

"Justin'll do what?" Justin's voice came from behind them. He joined the three of them.

"Rock climbing."

"I've tried that before. I suck. No balance whatsoever." He cranked his arm around Rachel's neck and squeezed. "This here's the athlete."

Payton couldn't have planned this better. Before he knew it, most of the team was huddling in on the discussion, laughing and jibing each other, and he found himself offering to take the entire team out for dinner and drinks again sometime soon.

"Rachel!" Meline yelled from his spot in the next bay. A sudden hush fell over the group. "Did you go over the stats on Pocono?"

Payton hadn't met the guy and already he hated him. Hugo didn't say anything, but his attention focused on Rachel. Payton caught Neil's gaze and signaled for him to cut the camera.

"Working on it." Rachel sounded completely calm.

"I need those by morning."

"I know."

Justin turned toward Meline and opened his mouth, but, and Payton was sure no one except him saw it, Hugo held him back with a tug on his shirt.

"You know—" Meline belligerently crossed his arms over his chest "—maybe if some of us took our jobs more seriously instead of doing interviews for *friends,* this team might be winning races." The shot was obviously directed toward Hugo about Rachel, and Meline had no sooner thrown the punch than he walked away.

Why Rachel didn't yell anything after him in defense of herself was beyond Payton. It took everything in him to hold himself back, but it wasn't his place. With the mood soured, the team dispersed in various directions. The last one to leave was Hugo.

"Don't say anything," Rachel said to Hugo before he left. "It's my battle."

"MELINE'S AN IDIOT," Payton said, later that same night.

"He's really not. He's a technical wiz, been in the business a very long time." Rachel sat back and brushed the ground-in dirt off her gloved hands. Her house was getting closer to completion and Payton had offered to help put in some finishing touches in the form of some color around the yard.

In her usual analytical, no-nonsense manner, she hadn't seemed to care overly much about the addition, but for a reason he refused to examine too closely he wanted her coming home to a house that looked lived-in and loved, a place that welcomed her with open arms at the end of a long workday.

They'd already arranged planters and hung baskets of flowers on the back deck. Now they were focusing on the front porch. Rachel had purchased two rocking chairs and a garden table and they'd arranged them in the larger space off to the left of the door. The porch was wide, so there was plenty of room for several planters of flowers in addition to a row of hanging baskets, filled with shade-loving plants.

"What if it is me?" she said. "What if I *have* been screwing up my brother's engines?"

"You haven't been ruining anything, and Meline knows it. You outsmart him, and he feels threatened."

"I swear this is all because of his divorce. He's taking it out on me. And I have to sit there and take it."

"No, you don't. Do something."

"I've tried talking to him. He won't listen to me."

"Does your uncle know that?"

She didn't say anything.

"Quit then. Go to another team." He watched the emotions play out on her face.

"Are you out of your mind?"

Probably. This was clearly none of his business. "Rachel, you're very talented and highly respected. A few phone calls and you'd be working for another team by Monday morning. With a promotion to boot."

"I'm a Murphy. I can't work for another crew chief. That'd break Hugo's heart."

"He doesn't seem to care right now, does he?" Payton didn't know why *he* should care so much. But he did. "Hugo told you to deal with it."

"If I ever want to be a crew chief, I have to learn to fight my own battles. Hugo has good intentions."

"Good intentions or not, by not checking Meline, your uncle's sending the message that he thinks Meline's right."

She seemed to consider what he was saying, but it wasn't enough. His frustration continued building. "Rachel, you graduated summa cum laude with a degree in engineering. If you can't work on the Fulcrum team, and you won't work for anyone else, then leave NASCAR altogether."

"Leave NASCAR?" She looked at him as if he'd grown an ear on his forehead.

"Go to work for one of the big auto makers. Better yet, make a clean break, and go into another field." What the hell was he saying? He knew what her answer would be.

"Payton, NASCAR's my life. I couldn't leave Fulcrum Racing any more than I could…solo Half Dome."

To hear her put it in those terms, his terms, left a sick feeling in his stomach. He had to look away. He'd be moving in a few months. He might never see her again. All because she was too tied in with this community, with these racing teams, with NASCAR. How could someone, anyone, be so set in her ways, so closed to other options?

"Have you ever considered that you might be hiding away here?" he said. "Using NASCAR and your family as cover?"

"Cover? What?"

"What other kind of life do you know, Rachel? How would you know if there's something else you'd rather do? What of the world have you seen that doesn't involve a race track?"

Her brows furrowed.

He had to open her eyes. He could see her doing so much, going so many places, if only she'd open her horizons. *And come with him.* He wanted her to wake up and come with him to L.A. "There's a big, wide world out there that you know nothing about." But she'd never even consider the possibility of leaving North Carolina. "You're sitting here, in this house, and you're settling because you don't know what else to do."

"How can you say that? I love my life, my family, my home."

"Love them, or need them?" He threw down his gloves. "Face it, you're not growing. You're not flourishing. You're hiding away here. You lock people out to protect yourself. You're stagnating. Dying. Suffocating."

She stared at him. As if she didn't know who he was. *No commitments. No claims.* He'd gone too far.

How had he gotten here?

Rachel's phone rang. Another time she might've ignored it. After what he'd said, she looked as if she needed to get away. She ran inside to answer the call, and when she came back out, her eyes were wide, her face pale.

"What happened?" Payton asked.

"That was Hugo. Kim's in the hospital."

CHAPTER FOURTEEN

PAYTON SCREECHED TO A STOP at the emergency entrance of the Charlotte hospital. "Go," he said. "I'll take care of the car."

Rachel jumped out, ran inside to find Justin and Hugo already at the visitor counter getting security passes. "I need one, too," she said to the officer.

"What happened?" she asked Hugo.

"She passed out at work, and they called an ambulance. That's all we know."

They snatched up their passes and headed through the security doors. Justin and Hugo whizzed by Rachel when she stopped outside Kim's room. Her hands were shaking, her skin clammy. If she went in there like this, she'd probably scare Kim.

"Rachel?" Her brother peeked around the corner. "You comin'?"

She stared into her brother's soft brown eyes. He was scared, too. She had to get hold of herself. For Justin and Hugo. And for Kim. When he reached out a hand, she took a deep breath and let him draw her into the room.

Surrounded by machines with various tubes sticking out of her arms, Kim sat, propped partway up, in the hospital bed. She smiled weakly when she spotted Rachel following Justin into the room. Hugo had sat in the chair on Kim's right and Justin stood near the end of the hospital bed.

"Hey, you." Rachel dropped into the only other chair immediately to Kim's left, a sense of panic, something deep-seated, something she couldn't name, threatening her composure. People died every day. Her parents were here one day, gone the next. Rachel knew the fear was irrational, but what if Kim was *really* sick, sick to the point of dying?

Don't leave me, Kim. Don't you ever leave.

"You guys came here empty-handed?" Kim's voice sounded quiet and breathy. "What's a girl gotta do to get some flowers?"

She may have lost more weight since Rachel last saw her and her skin was nearly as pale as the wall behind her, but Kim obviously hadn't lost her sense of humor. And she was still as beautiful as ever.

"You're not supposed to be in here," Rachel said, and Kim managed a feeble smile. Justin was usually the one they worried about.

"Goes to show," Kim whispered, her eyes growing heavy, "driving a stock car isn't nearly as dangerous as stem-cell research."

Justin chuckled. "Anytime you want to take over, coz, the No. 448's all yours."

"I'll get right on it." Kim's voice sounded groggy.

Hugo put his head down. Listening to the three of them banter back and forth usually put a smile on his face. Not today. Today, he barely held back tears.

"I'll be okay, Daddy." Kim rubbed her thumb over his hand. "You concentrate on winning in Michigan, okay?" She closed her eyes and drifted off to sleep. Rachel lowered the head of the bed and planted a soft kiss on her cousin's forehead.

The doctor strode into the room. "I'm your E.R. physician." He reviewed Kim's chart. "I'll be in charge of Kim until we get her stabilized and moved into a regular room in the hospital."

"Hugo Murphy. Kim's father." He stood and shook the doctor's hand. "These are Kim's cousins, Rachel and Justin. Do you have a few minutes to tell us what's going on?"

"Absolutely." He nodded.

Hugo motioned toward the hall so they could let Kim sleep, and they filed out of the room.

"Will she be all right?" Rachel asked.

"Kim's in the advanced stages of Chronic Kidney Disease, or CKD. I'm guessing that her kidneys haven't been functioning properly for some time. There's a great deal of scarring."

"How'd this happen?" Justin asked. "Why?"

"The most common causes are diabetes and untreated hypertension. Does she have a history of either?"

"Not that I know of." Hugo looked to Rachel.

Rachel shook her head. "Up until about six months ago she has always been pretty healthy."

The doctor refocused on Hugo. "Do you or your family members have a history of kidney disease?"

"Kim's my adopted daughter," he explained. "She was about three when her birth mom and I got married, and we'd only been married for a year when Sylvie up and left. I honestly don't remember the woman's medical history."

"Knowing her history is more for peace of mind than anything. Regardless of the cause of Kim's condition, her treatment remains the same. We still need the results from a few tests, but, with any luck, we'll have her stabilized and ready to go home in a week or two."

"Then what? She'll be cured?"

"She's in the advanced stages of CKD. Unfortunately, she'll need ongoing dialysis."

"For how long?"

The doctor shook his head. "For now, let's focus on stabilizing Kim. Later, you'll be working with a kidney specialist to determine her treatment."

"How long?" her uncle pushed.

"For as long as it works." The doctor hesitated for the first time in their conversation. "Eventually, she'll need a kidney transplant."

"People get kidney transplants every day, though," Hugo said. "She'll live a normal life, right?"

"We're getting ahead of ourselves here." He paused again. "Kim may be placed on a national register for a kidney, and if we can find a suitable donor, her prognosis is good."

Oh, God.

"If?" Hugo prodded. "Why wouldn't we be able to find a donor? Hell, you can take one of my kidneys. Lay me out. Right now. Today. Take mine."

"Or one of mine," Rachel said.

"Or mine," Justin added.

The doctor's smile was understanding, but grim. "I'm sure all of you can and will be tested, but I must warn you Kim's blood type is rare. There are several factors that need to fall into place for a good donor match. The chances of finding a match within the general population are extremely low."

"So what does that mean? She's gonna die?"

Rachel felt light-headed and leaned against her brother.

"The best chance for a match with Kim is from someone in her immediate family. Can you contact her mother?"

"I don't believe this." Hugo put his head down for a moment.

"We don't know where Sylvie is," Justin said.

Hugo took a deep breath, calming himself. "I haven't seen hide nor hair of Sylvie since the day she left. I have no clue where she's at."

"Then all we can do is wait for a match to appear on the national register."

"How much time do we have?"

"That, I don't know." The doctor closed his file. "For now let's focus on stabilizing Kim and finding her a room for her stay at the hospital." He walked down the hall toward the nurses' station.

Rachel looked from Hugo to Justin and back again, tears resurfacing.

Suddenly angry, her uncle clenched his jaw. "I'm hiring a private investigator. We have to find Sylvie. She might be Kim's only chance." He went back into Kim's room.

Rachel sighed and propped herself against the wall.

"You okay?" Justin asked.

She shook her head. "I can't believe this is happening."

"She's gonna be okay. Either there's a donor out there, or Hugo'll find Sylvie."

Rachel felt her world spinning. She wrapped her arms around herself, holding things together. One by one, pieces flew away. She was a little girl again, wondering why Mama and Daddy had left her.

"What happens if she dies, Justin? Everyone dies around us."

He didn't say anything. What could he say?

"Don't you ever wonder why Mama killed herself?"

"She was sick, Rachel. If they knew then what they know now about postpartum depression, she might still be alive."

"What about Daddy? A hit-and-run. So soon after Mama. Why? How do you make sense of that?"

"I don't. Rach, you'll go crazy if you keep thinking about that stuff. Stop it," he whispered.

"Don't you ever worry about everyone leaving you?"

He hugged her. "No one's leaving anybody, Rachel. It's gonna be okay."

"You don't know that." She shrugged away from him. "It might not be okay. Kim might die." What if they all left her? Hugo, Justin, Kim? They were her world. All she had. More pieces flew away. Before she knew it, there'd be nothing left of her. She had to stop it. "I don't think I can do this."

"Oh, Rach." He made a soft, sad sound. "What's your alternative? You gonna walk away from Kim? Turn your back on her? She might be your cousin on paper, but she's more a sister to both of us. What about me and Hugo? You gonna cut us out of your life, too? I'd like to see you try."

Fast-moving footsteps sounded from down the hall. Her brother glanced around and his jaw clenched as he held back tears. Sophia Grosso.

Rachel's cheeks heated. What was she doing here? She stiffened. Justin walked away from Rachel, opened his arms to Sophia and wrapped them around her so tightly there wasn't a crack of air between them.

"I came as soon as I heard," Sophia whispered into his chest. "Had to pull a few strings to get back here."

"I'm so glad you did." He closed his eyes and buried his face in Sophia's long blond hair.

Rachel swallowed back her anger. This was her brother's choice and she had to accept it, or risk pushing him away. There was so much love there.

Love.

Oh God. She had to get out of here. Through the maze of hallways, she found her way back to the waiting area, pushed through the doors and headed for fresh air.

"Rachel!" Payton jumped up from a chair in the corner.

She took several steps and ran straight into his arms. She'd forgotten he was here. Her friend. Such a close friend in such a short amount of time. It was so good to feel him around her, holding her, supporting her.

"You all right?"

She nodded.

"Kim?"

"She has kidney disease and will eventually need a transplant." She didn't want to think about it. Too much to absorb.

She stepped back and looked into his eyes. Mistake. He cared. Too much. Their conversation back at her house came back in a blast, making her feel raw all over again. He thought she was crazy for not wanting to leave North Carolina, for being so tied into her family. He wanted her to leave NASCAR.

She didn't need to leave. Payton was the one who didn't belong here. This was none of his business. Rachel might not be capable of pushing her brother away, any more than she could blow off Hugo or Kim. But she sure as hell didn't need to let anyone else in.

She jumped away from him. "Thanks for the ride, but you need to go."

"Rachel? What's the matter?"

"You shouldn't have stayed. That's all."

"Sorry. I thought I'd make sure Kim was okay. See if you needed anything."

"I thought the limits on our relationship were clear."

He clenched his jaw. "Maybe you should refresh my memory."

"You know what I'm talking about." She stepped back. "No claims. No commitments. No expectations." Another step back. "What happens to Kim, Justin, Hugo—or me—is none of your business. You're a diversion, Payton. You're not a part of my life." She ran outside and kept on running.

CHAPTER FIFTEEN

PAYTON HADN'T SEEN or spoken with Rachel since the hospital incident, and if he could get through this weekend's race in Michigan he'd be in the clear for a while. The next several races, California, New Hampshire and Daytona, were too far from Charlotte for his station to foot the travel bill. And with her crazy work schedule it was doubtful he'd see her anytime soon without making a concerted effort.

Though he couldn't help but wonder how this weekend was going for her. He'd heard Johnny Meline had graced the Fulcrum team with his presence and Kim might be spending the day at the track. Rachel was bound to be completely preoccupied.

Payton kept his head down anyway. He needed some distance and perspective. She'd been right, of course. He hadn't belonged at the hospital. Kim's illness was a family matter, and while he might be a friend, he was still a reporter. He had no right getting involved in the lives of the people he interviewed.

Understanding that didn't make what she'd said hurt any less. What confused and confounded him more than anything was that what Rachel said *had* cut, surprisingly deep.

He'd been careless. He understood that now. He'd gotten so engrossed in doing these NASCAR family specials that he'd let himself get wrapped up in people's lives, especially Rachel's, and had begun to feel a part of NASCAR.

What difference should it make to Payton if Dean Grosso had beat out his son by coming in first at Dover? Why should Payton care if Bart and Will Branch's father was missing and had been accused of embezzling money from his company? Maybe all the ongoing family drama had caused Bart to hit the wall at Pocono and wipe out six other drivers. First, the rumor was Gideon Taney was selling the MMG team, then he wasn't, then he was getting married. And he'd heard through the grapevine that Kim was doing remarkably better. So what? Payton had no right to care.

But he did.

Somewhere along the way this NASCAR stuff had seeped under his skin. The drivers, the teams, the track staff, all good people. No one had gotten to him more than Rachel. Truth was, he missed her. Missed talking with her, listening to her, watching her. Being with her.

He couldn't afford to care.

His Grosso special was running today and if preliminary station reaction was any gauge at all, viewers would love it. He'd finally gotten his interview with the elusive Rachel Murphy. People were already talking about him and his big coup and floundering to get their own interviews with Rachel.

She'd turned them all down.

Once he put the finishing touches on the Murphy family special, his station's ratings were bound to increase. He was on his way.

"You ready?" Payton asked Neil.

"Always." Neil nodded. "You okay today, Payton?"

"Fine. Let's go."

"Camera's on."

The Branch twins were planning on meeting with him right before today's race. Payton was lucky. The twins came out of the drivers' meeting together. "Bart. Will." Payton extended his hand. "How are you guys doing today?"

"Perfect."

"Great."

They nodded their blond, curly heads.

"If you guys didn't have on your sponsor duds, I wouldn't be able to tell you two apart."

They both laughed, and Payton kept the conversation going from there. The two brothers were open and honest and funny. All of it good stuff. Could go right into his special with minor editing.

He glanced past the Branches and caught his breath.

A hundred, no, probably two hundred feet away, there was Rachel, a smile on her face. Kim had, indeed, made it to the track. Justin was pushing her in a wheelchair and Hugo was walking next to them, but the four of them looked happy.

He spun around to Neil. "Gimme that camera."

"What?"

"Camera." Payton seized it out of Neil's hands. "Sorry guys," he said to the Branch twins. "Gimme a minute."

"No problem."

He focused in on the Murphys and the kind of family shot a cameraman couldn't stage if he tried. They made a complete picture, the four of them together talking and laughing. He visualized Sophia Grosso in the frame, holding Justin's hand. She was a stretch but she'd fit. Payton, on the other hand, was another story altogether.

Rachel had been right. She'd reminded him of something he'd forgotten for a moment. Payton was a diversion to her. Nothing more, nothing less. Wanting to have sex with her didn't mean he belonged in that picture along with her family.

He should be used to diversions. Hell, his whole life was one big distraction after another. Instead, a strange feeling shot through him. Something he couldn't remember ever feeling for a woman. His heart raced, his thoughts scattered, his cheeks felt heated. What? Why?

That little outburst of his at her house before they'd found out about Kim being in the hospital? He couldn't believe what he'd said to her. *There's a big, wide world out there that you know nothing about. You're sitting here, in this house, and you're settling because you don't know what else to do.*

What a trip. He realized it now. He'd been mad, still was, at Rachel. At her inability to see outside her own limits. At her unwillingness to open her eyes. She wouldn't even consider the possibility of moving to California with him. And that made him mad, that someone could be so closed to possibilities.

Had he ever before cared enough about a woman to actually get angry? Maybe once or twice. More important, had he ever cared enough about a woman to want her to head around the world with him? Never.

"IT'S SO GOOD TO BE HOME," Kim said over the phone to Rachel. "I slept great last night." She sounded rested, too, this morning.

Michigan had been a challenge for Kim, not to mention worrisome for Hugo, but she'd wanted to prove to everyone that she could keep up with an occasional race and the next several scheduled tracks were even farther from Charlotte.

It had been just Rachel's luck that Johnny Meline had chosen yesterday's race to attend. Michigan had been entirely uneventful, so Meline had, of course, maintained that there was nothing wrong with his engines. Big surprise, that.

"Do you need anything?" Rachel cupped the phone between her ear and shoulder and finished making her bed.

"Nope. My refrigerator's stuffed to the gills thanks to you. I have the stack of books and movies Justin dropped off. And Daddy's coming by later to take me to dialysis."

"Your boss isn't giving you a hard time about missing work, is he?"

"Everyone's been very supportive. Promise."

Rachel sat down on the edge of her bed, picked up her skipping stone from the top of her nightstand and rubbed it between her fingers. "Are you sure you won't change your mind and stay with me for a while?"

"In that construction mess? Are you out of your mind?"

"I can have Harlan hold off on any more work for a few weeks."

"I'm *fine,* Rachel," Kim whispered. "Quit worrying."

Kim had almost died, and Rachel should pretend it never happened. The best she could hope for was not panicking again as she had in the hospital, but that had been a completely normal reaction for that kind of family crisis. What was she supposed to be, made out of stone? That she loved her family didn't mean she was stagnating, *or* suffocating as Payton had claimed.

"Let me know if you need anything. Okay?"

"Will do."

Rachel hung up the phone, sat back against her pillows and flipped her rock in the air like a coin. She loved Lake Norman and this house. That didn't mean she wasn't growing. She earned good money, loved her job, traveled all over the country. Heck, she knew plenty of people who never left the state of North Carolina except for races at Martinsville, Bristol or Talladega.

Who did Payton think he was, anyway, lecturing her on how to live her life? Because she'd found her niche in NASCAR first lap off the starting line didn't mean it wasn't right for her. Because she hadn't floundered her life away chasing one summit after another like one particular person she knew didn't mean she hadn't found her true passion.

Since when was being happy a crime?

She slapped the stone on top of her nightstand and stood. Her gaze shifted to the bottom drawer of her bedside table. Was she happy? Then why hadn't she touched those books since Harlan had brought them over?

She opened the drawer, pulled out what appeared to be diaries and glanced inside the first cover. Her mother's penmanship was fluid and simple, with perfectly formed letters, and it was strange imagining a dead person having written all these pages. Her mother had dated each entry, like a journal. Rachel plopped herself down on the floor, put the books in order and began reading the earliest one.

Many of the entries were filled with mundane details of her days, her friendships, her family. So-and-so said this, so-and-so did that. Things that made her happy, things that made her sad. Hopes, dreams, fantasies. None of it was earth-shattering. None of it seemed out of the ordinary, until Rachel got to the end of the second book. That's when her mother, Ginny Cooper, had met Troy Murphy.

It was no different than reading the sappiest romance tale ever written. The story was sad and predictable to the point of being completely clichéd. Her mother was a hopeless romantic and her daddy a carousing ladies' man who'd finally been tamed.

Only Rachel already knew this story didn't have a happily-ever-after ending, so everything she read, even the sweetest, happiest entries were tainted with reality. Ginny believed she could change Troy, satisfy him, make him happy, keep him home. She learned how to cook his favorite meals, agonized over gaining weight with her pregnancy and lost confidence in her appearance.

The whole story made Rachel angry. At both her mother and father. How could they have both been so ignorant and selfish?

In the middle of the fourth book, Rachel was born, and the tone of her mother's writing changed. Dramatically.

> *Rachel. Troy's not sure if he likes the name.*
> *But I don't care what he says.*

> *I honestly don't know how I ever lived without this baby. My life meant nothing before this. When I hold her, and she looks at me with those big, beautiful eyes, I know what love is. Troy says I'm going to spoil her. How can you spoil a baby? That's just plain silly.*

> *For the first time in my life, I know who I am, why I'm here.*

There isn't a more perfect baby in all the world.

The journals went on and on with details of Rachel's first year and, with every passage, her throat constricted more tightly with emotion. The answer to one of the questions that had been plaguing her for years was there in every word on every page, so clear, it was almost blinding with intensity. Rachel had been loved. With everything her mother had to give. Then she got pregnant again.

It's a boy, I know it. So different from when I was pregnant with Rachel. I'm carrying him so low, I have to pee all the time.

I think Troy's feelings were hurt that Rachel's been saying "Mama" for months now and not much else. Justin won't even go to him, and he cries every time Troy tries to pick him up. He's never around, what can he expect?

Troy hasn't taken me out dancing for months, let alone out to dinner. Justin won't go to sleep for a babysitter. He's a mama's boy, everyone says. As if that's the worst thing in the world.

Troy rocked Justin to sleep today, and it was the sweetest thing I've ever seen.

Rachel said "Daddy" today for the first time and you shoulda seen Troy smile. He was so proud. When he looked at me that smile warmed me through and through.

He still loves me. I don't care what anybody says. They're all jealous. I wish they'd leave us alone.

Sometimes I hate this house. I hate this lake.

I wanna go home. But Mama says I never shoulda married Troy Murphy, pregnant or not. Everyone knew he was bad news. Daddy says I got exactly what I asked for.

I can't go home. I can't stay here.

Sometimes I want to go to sleep and never wake up.

Tomorrow's another day, right? It'll be better. It has to be better.

If the kids would sleep through the night, I think everything would be okay. If it's not Justin up, it's Rachel. If it's not Rachel, it's Justin. Every night.

Troy promised he'd come home right after work and take care of the babies. He promised.

I'm a bad mother.

I fell asleep at the kitchen table. When I woke up, Justin was playing in his crib, but I couldn't find Rachel. She got herself out of the house and went down by the lake.

If anything ever happened to her, I'd never forgive myself.

I can't do this anymore. I can't be here. I'm sorry. Rachel. Justin. My sweet, sweet babies. I'm so sorry. It'll be better this way. I promise.

Rachel's tears splashed on the old paper, and that's when she noticed the old water stains already at the bottom of the page. Mama had cried, too. Right on this page. The last page her mother had written. That realization made her sob more. She didn't bother to stop, simply grabbed a box of tissues and cried.

After a while, she took a deep breath and rubbed her cheeks dry. She closed the last book, its pages only half-filled with journal entries, and carefully placed all of them back in the bottom drawer of her nightstand. She reached for her stone. Someday, if her brother wanted the books, they'd be here, but Rachel had read all she needed.

There were no secrets hidden in those pages. Her mama and daddy were young people who'd fallen in love, lived their lives as best as they'd known how and made a lot of mistakes. They were human. And frail. Her mother may have chosen to swallow those sleeping pills, but her thoughts, what had been driving her actions, had not been voluntary at all.

Ginny Cooper Murphy had loved her children. That's all Rachel needed to know. That's all there was to know.

The stone felt cool in her hand. Funny, she still wasn't ready to let it go.

CHAPTER SIXTEEN

PAYTON OPENED THE HEAVY DOORS to WJAZ's main offices near downtown Charlotte and breezed through the front lobby. "Good morning, Annette." He raised a hand in salute to the matronly receptionist.

"Morning, Payton." She raised her eyebrows at him over the top of her reading glasses. "Jay's already asked for you twice this morning."

That probably meant the answer to Payton's second request for travel to Texas for some background work on the Branches was a no-go. "Thanks for the heads-up."

He went through the staff doors and headed into the cool, dimly lit bowels of the old building. Artificial lighting was more manageable than its natural counterpart, so all of the studios and editing rooms were in the center of the building. After one or two turns in the narrow halls, he cut through a general staff area in hopes of avoiding Jay and went into his dimly lit, windowless office.

Jay must have been watching for him. He walked in, practically on Payton's heels. "We're getting calls left and right on your Grosso show that aired last weekend," he said, before Payton had the chance to sit down.

"Good? Bad?" People rarely took time out for indifference.

"Mostly great. A few thought you spent too much time on Kent and could've focused more on Dean."

"Can't please 'em all."

"Initial estimates are that ratings increased more than five points."

Payton shot a look at his boss. "Really?" Five points was big. The fact that they'd been able to relate it to the Grosso special was even bigger.

Jay nodded. "And that's not the best part."

"What could be better than that?"

"NSN picked it up."

NSN? In a state of disbelief, Payton slipped down in front of his editing equipment. This was better than any of his wildest dreams. He'd never imagined that NSN would appreciate his work enough to buy the rights from WJAZ and air the program nationally.

"You did good." Jay slapped him on the back. "I want to see more of the same on the Murphys and the Branches. Go ahead and make that trip to Dallas." His boss slid the glass door to Payton's office closed.

Payton stared at his blank screen, absorbing the news. Now every national network would have the opportunity to see his work and NSN, in particular, would be keeping an eye out for him. His mind raced at the possibilities as he loaded the tapes from the last several days onto his computer.

He'd have to do a good job on the Branch show, but no way was he going to focus on the scandal surrounding the family. The tabloids had that covered. He flipped through several files on the family and loaded them onto his screen. After he got a few clips in Texas, all the pieces would slip into place. Funny, wealthy Texans. What was there not to like?

The Murphys, though, would make or break him, and it was taking some time and planning to create something special, something different. He was extremely late but it would be worth it. If he did their family right, he had a feeling he'd be able to practically write his own contract with a national network.

He loaded a clip he'd taken of Rachel and watched it. She was incredibly photogenic. He loaded a few more. And a few more. By the time he'd finished, it became obvious that he had four times the material on her than he did on Hugo, or Justin, for that matter. He watched each one of them several times, putting possible combinations of scenes together in his mind.

Sometime later, his office door slowly slid open. "Want some help with that editing?" Neil asked.

"No, thanks." *These are my babies.*

"Suit yourself." The door slid closed again.

It took hours to find the right music. Some hard-core rock for an upbeat charge and some instrumentals for the softer, more emotional moments. Several more hours laying the sound over the video. He bought a sandwich from the cafeteria and ate lunch at his desk. Before he knew it, his co-workers were heading home for the day and he'd only, at best, drafted the first ten minutes of the Murphy show.

He froze a frame on Rachel's face. This clip was at Fulcrum headquarters. She was laughing at something Fred Dooley had said. He could see the admiration and respect on Fred's face.

God, she was beautiful. Sweet. Full of emotion. If he could capture the Rachel he knew and project it onto the screen, this station's racing audience would stand and jump for joy. She was NASCAR's darling and they didn't even know it. Yet.

He stared into those expressive hazel eyes and an odd feeling of emptiness gripped him. He pushed it away. Rachel was a means to an end, a way to help make this sportscaster's dreams come true. Nothing more, nothing less.

"HUGO?" Rachel opened the door to the conference room and stopped. Pitch-blackness engulfed her. She saw nothing except for the glow from the brilliant white and clear blue image on the flat-screened TV at the front of the room.

Gradually, her eyes adjusted and she noticed the whole team seated around the table, completely silent. The only sound came from the TV, the breathing of the man climbing an ice-and-snow-covered mountain.

"Sit down." Justin yanked her down onto the chair next to him. "You gotta watch this."

She stared at the screen. "Who is that?" But she felt the answer before the question left her mouth.

"It's Payton," her brother whispered. "On the climb he did that documentary on. Remember the one he told us about? *National Geographic* picked it up."

"I remember." She was still mad at Payton, or hurt, probably both. She hadn't called him and he hadn't called her. Maybe their friendship had been nothing more than a blip in her life. Maybe it was best that way. He'd be gone soon, anyway.

"Is that Cerro Torre?" she asked.

"I think so. In the Patagonia Mountains in South America."

"Shh!" came the general consensus of the viewers.

"Where'd you find the DVD?" she whispered.

"Hugo found it," Justin whispered in her ear. "He's been checking out your boy."

Her boy. Payton, his face covered with whiskers, ice and snow, was barely recognizable, but those eyes, a shade darker than the sky behind him, were unmistakable.

After climbing with him, she now knew enough to understand what was happening in the video. Enough to know the risks they were taking. Whoever was belaying Payton had a camera and was filming his ascent.

Whack! Payton slammed his pick into a wall of ice, once, twice, three times. "This ice sucks," Payton said. The brittle sound of ice cracking boomed across the surround-sound system. "Hold on, Brian."

More cracking. Wind. Whooshing. His pieces anchored into the ice gave way and Payton should have fallen. Instead, he landed his pick in solid, hard ice and the crampons at his feet miraculously held. Her shoulders tensed as she watched him searching for another anchor for his rope.

"There," Payton said, sounding winded and tired as he clipped the rope through the carabiner. "We've gone four thousand vertical feet. Ten more to the summit. That overhang of ice up there doesn't look good."

She couldn't take her eyes off the screen.

"We don't make it this time," the other guy yelled, "it's over. We'll have to head back down to base camp."

"Now you know why this was considered the hardest climb in the world for years."

Slowly, painstakingly, Payton made his way over the ice overhang and to the summit and then took his turn belaying his partner. Once they'd both finally made it to the summit, the other man sat the camera down, still filming. Wind whistled in the background as the two men laughed and hollered. They seemed too winded and tired to hug or slap each other on the backs.

"Like winning a race," Hugo murmured.

The entire conference room fell silent as Payton panned the camera past the vista surrounding him. Heavy white clouds moved below in an almost straight line. Jagged, snow-covered mountain peaks surrounded him and a deep valley lay off in the distance with what looked like glacial ice giving way to the huge lake or river.

"Six months of training and preparations," Payton said, his voice cut by the biting winds. "One week to base camp, five days waiting out the weather, two failed attempts and three days climbing to get here."

"That isn't winning one race," Justin said. "That's an entire season there. Like winning the championship."

Rachel imagined the kind of determination and motivation it would take for a person to successfully complete a climbing expedition, the resilience a person would need to stand again and walk after the kind of paralyzing fall Payton had experienced.

"What do you think, Rachel?" Justin leaned toward her and whispered, "Maybe this guy deserves more than a measly taste testing, huh?"

CHAPTER SEVENTEEN

"COME ON, DADDY. Let's go." Catie charged the ticket booth at the New Hampshire race track and bent her head toward the attendant behind the glass window. "Rachel Murphy left some tickets here for us." She spoke Rachel's name with reverence and awe, as if she were referring to none other than the Queen of England. "We're the Stroms."

The ticket lady pointed toward another building. "Credentials are held in the registration area."

"Huh?" She may as well have been speaking Greek to Harlan. This confirmed one of the reasons he'd avoided asking for pit passes from Hugo all these years. These tracks were so large and the rules so involved, it made Harlan's head spin.

"Over here." Catie grabbed his arm and pulled him along.

This was her dream. What could he do but follow his daughter around and catch her if she fell? Or, worse, be there to commiserate if Rachel dropped her number one fan directly onto her head.

Overall though, Harlan was glad he'd taken Rachel's offer to share the plane ride with the Fulcrum team, but once they'd landed, he'd made sure that he and Catie had headed off on their own and given the Murphys plenty of time to take care of business. He and Catie had rented a car and were staying at a hotel and doing a few touristy things. They hadn't been on a vacation in years, and he was actually enjoying himself.

After a short while, the people in the registration area gave them tickets to Sunday's race, sold out to a crowd of fans, and something called credentials good for the entire weekend. They walked through the security gates, their hot passes that Rachel had gotten for them hanging from their necks, hoping to watch a few qualifying runs.

He only hoped the weather would hold, but the sky promised nothing. When the wind accelerated, he said a prayer. *This is your baby's day, Lynnie. Help make it a good one for her.*

"Come on, Daddy." Catie took off toward the infield. To say she'd been ecstatic the entire morning would have been an understatement. This had been all she'd talked about for the last week. "I want to see everything."

They walked the long line of haulers, and up and down pit road. Catie talked to anyone and everyone who looked even remotely approachable. She absorbed the smells, the sounds and the faces as if she were gulping down her first meal in days. "Saved the best for last. Let's find the Fulcrum garage." They took a walk past the open stalls.

"Hey, Harlan!" It was Hugo's voice.

Harlan glanced inside the garage area and saw his friend sitting beside a tool chest next to the No. 448 car, hood propped open and the front end jacked.

"There they are!" Catie almost jumped up and down.

"Be careful, honey. Don't touch anything." Harlan moved tentatively toward Hugo. Several of the Fulcrum team members were milling around the car, including Justin and Wade, the car chief. Based on the size of the feet sticking out from under the car, it appeared Rachel was under there doing something.

"Well, hello again, Miss Catie," Hugo said. He was sitting back, fairly relaxed, his arms crossed over his chest. "It's about time you talked your daddy into bringing you to a track. I've been bugging him for years."

"You know I don't like being in the way," Harlan said.

"That could never happen, old friend. It's good to have you here." Hugo introduced Harlan and Catie to the team.

"What are you guys working on?" Unlike most other girls, Catie didn't go all goo-goo over Justin. Harlan felt kind of proud of that, but part of him wished she were a little more ordinary. Catie craned her neck for a view under the hood, studied the car engine and, Harlan would've sworn, started drooling.

"We took a few practice runs," Justin said. "Rachel's adjusting the sway bars again."

Rachel rolled out from under the car, her face lined with concentration. "Hi, Harlan," she said absently. "Oh. Hi, Catie." She glanced at Catie, but seemed to stare straight through her. "Wade, we need to adjust the camber on that right front tire."

"Yeah, I've got it down," Wade said.

Now that Harlan thought about it, this was probably a bad time for Catie to connect with everyone, especially Rachel, focused as she was on qualifying. "Catie, maybe we should come back after qualifying is over."

"But, Daddy, I want to watch 'em work on the car."

"You're fine, Harlan, don't worry about it," Hugo said.

Catie's shoulders sagged. "Daddy's right, though, you gotta kick ass in qualifying, 'specially at this track. Once the race starts, those tight turns make it hard to pass."

"You are absolutely correct about that, Miss Catie," Hugo said. "When are you graduating from college so you can come work for me?"

Catie grinned and went to the other side of the car.

Harlan glared at Hugo and whispered, "Don't encourage her."

"Why not?" Hugo whispered back. "Your daughter's not only got passion for something, she just might have the talent necessary to turn that passion into a career. How is she ever going to know if she doesn't try?"

"You don't get it. Rachel's not your daughter."

Hugo glared back at him. "I've been raising that girl since she was two. She's as much my daughter as Kim. You're an old-fashioned fool."

Frustrated, Harlan stepped outside the garage and took a deep breath of hot, humid air.

"What's gotten into you, Harlan?" Hugo asked, joining him.

"I don't know, but it's more than being old-fashioned."

"What, then?"

Harlan wished he knew. A stiff breeze blew past and he tugged his hat lower on his brow.

"Don't you want Catie to be happy?" Hugo asked.

"'Course I want her to be happy."

"What are you worried about?"

Then it hit Harlan, why all this car and engine and engineering nonsense was bothering him. "I don't want her to be alone, Hugo." Tears misted his eyes, and he quickly blinked them away. "Like me. Like Rachel."

"And me." Hugo sighed. "There are worse things than being alone."

"Name one."

"Hatin' your job." Hugo smacked him on the back. "Besides, you, me and Rachel? The three of us have chosen to be alone, in one way or another."

"It's looking like Catie might be making that same choice. I've screwed up, Hugo. She's never had a date. Heck, she's never even had a crush."

"That you know of. She might not tell you stuff like that. Kim and Rachel never told me. Catie's only fifteen. A lot can happen in the next few years. Look at Rachel. It's entirely possible she won't be alone much longer."

"That sportscaster I've seen hanging around?"

Hugo crossed his fingers. "That make her a better role model for your Catie?"

"It's a start." Harlan pulled himself together. "Think you could tie an apron on Rachel, get someone to teach her to cook?"

"I won't be holding my breath for that one." Hugo chuckled. "But I'm still awfully proud of her."

"DARN IT!" Fred swatted down his clipboard as a strong wind blew through the garage, ruffling more than papers "Quick! Grab that printout."

Justin took a second away from his conversation with the driver in the next garage stall to flatten down the papers. Hugo was talking with Harlan. Wade was talking with Harlan's daughter, Catie. And Rachel wished everyone would get out of her garage so she could get the tire camber adjusted properly.

The weather forecasters had predicted no rain, but this constant buffeting of wind was getting on everyone's nerves, especially Rachel's. She wished the sky would dump on them all and get it over with.

Focus. You have to get this right. She leaned over the fender, trying to adjust the camber. For the fifth time.

"Rachel?" Hugo's voice was soft, but commanding.

She stood up.

"Camber is not your responsibility," he said softly. "You want to be crew chief, you gotta learn how to back off and let your team do their jobs."

She glanced at Loren, their tire specialist. He was competent, that wasn't her problem. Her problem was thinking she could do everything better.

"It's called delegating," Hugo went on. "If you can't trust your team, you're in trouble."

Her uncle was right. "Loren?" she said.

He glanced up at her, a smile on his face. "Yes, ma'am?"

"Could you fix the camber, please? I shouldn't have tried in the first place."

"For sure." He had it finished in no time. "Okay. Let's pop the tire back on." A quick zap on the lug nuts with the air wrench and Loren had the tire back on, something she probably hadn't needed to take off anyway, and the No. 448 car was ready to go.

"Justin," she said. "You're all set for more practice runs around the track."

Hugo nodded his encouragement at Rachel as Loren and Fred pushed the car out of the garage. Justin climbed inside and headed out to the track.

You're hiding away here. You lock people out to protect yourself.

Payton's accusation bounced around inside her head. He was wrong. He had to be. She had a good life. She was satisfied. Happy even. Most of the time. Everyone had ups and downs and just because she was having problems with Meline, with a small part of her life, didn't mean she had to throw everything away.

What rubbed the most was that his opinion mattered.

"I get my driver's license next month," Catie said, coming to stand next to Rachel.

"Cool," Rachel said.

"Me and a friend have been rebuilding an engine."

"Good for you."

"We've done everything the manuals have said. Followed everything by the letter. Went back and checked. Double-checked. Triple-checked."

Rachel only half heard the kid.

"And the engine still won't turn over. No matter what we do."

"Bummer."

"Rachel, do you think you could... Is there any chance... Could you take a look at it?"

"I'm awfully busy, Catie."

"I know. There's no rush. I mean, I was hoping to take it out for my sixteenth birthday, but I can wait."

"Excuse me." The sound of a man's voice came from the hauler side of their bay.

Everyone in the garage looked up. A tall, attractive guy with a *Sports Illustrated* ID in his lanyard stood inside Fulcrum's garage space. Another reporter. Great. Since the media had found out she'd given Payton an interview, they'd been hounding her left and right.

"They said the media center was this way, but I can't seem to find it." An East Coast guy. The inflections in his accent sounded loud and clear.

"It's down there." Rachel pointed south. "I think it's right after the last garage."

He glanced past the building and grimaced. "Been that way three times."

"I heard someone say the track folks were having problems with some of the signs in this wind," Loren offered.

"If you say so," he said, sounding dejected and making no move to go.

Get out of my garage. "Here. I'll show you." She stepped outside, wanting nothing more than to get rid of him.

"Appreciate it."

"Whatever."

"You're Rachel Murphy, aren't you?"

Here we go. "Yep."

"Nice to meet you."

She nodded, trying to be polite.

"I don't get a chance to see a lot of the races, with my schedule and all," he said, "but I hear your brother's been having a tough stretch."

His schedule? "You're not a reporter?" She took another look at the ID dangling from his lanyard.

"Naw. They got me this pass today, wanting to thank me for an interview." He flicked his credentials. "I play football in the NFL."

Interesting. Rachel glanced at his left hand, her taste buds at full alert. No ring. "Where do you live?"

"Outside Boston. Born and raised here in New Hampshire, though."

"Really." She smiled. "Ever been to North Carolina?"

"Sure. Hotter than blazes. Don't know how you Southerners stand it. I'll take blizzards any day over those hurricanes."

Her wheels turned.

And just as quickly came to a full stop. She didn't know this guy's name, and she was doing it again, getting ready to work out her taste buds on another flavor. This couldn't be right, or emotionally healthy.

At the last garage, she pointed. "That's the media tent over there."

"Thanks, Rachel." He took a step or two and said, "Hey, do you want to catch some dinner after the race?"

He was probably nice. Uncomplicated. Perfect fling material. "Thanks, but I've got other plans."

"Maybe we'll run into each other again sometime."

"Maybe."

Rachel turned back toward the Fulcrum garage, and Payton's accusations hit like a heavy biscuit in her gut. She had been sheltering and distancing herself. Turned out, he knew her better than she knew herself.

Loren and Fred studied her as she stepped back into the garage. "What's the matter, Rachel?" Fred asked.

"You guys are both married, aren't you?"

They nodded, in turn.

"Have kids?"

"Yep," Loren said.

"Why?" Fred asked.

"Harlan?" she asked. "When's my house going to be finished?"

"A week. Worst case," he said.

"Why?" Hugo narrowed his eyes.

"I'm having a party. To celebrate my house being finished," she announced to the entire garage. That way she couldn't take it back. It wasn't much, but it was a start. If working on stock cars had taught her anything, it was that small adjustments could lead to big results. "And

everyone here, and your families, are all invited." She
glanced over at Harlan's daughter. "You, too, Catie."

Catie shrugged.

Rachel hadn't meant to, but she'd obviously really
bummed the kid out. *You're hiding away here. You lock
people out to protect yourself.* "Catie, when do you
turn sixteen?"

"In two weeks."

"We've got to get that car running for you, don't
we?" Rachel's heart raced, but she had to do this. "Can
I come over to your house Tuesday night to take a peek
at that engine?"

CHAPTER EIGHTEEN

"I'M IN THE PARK CITIES AREA, within the heart of Dallas, Texas." Under the early-evening shade of a tall cedar elm, Payton walked toward Neil, the camera light blaring red, indicating he was filming. "What do these upscale neighborhoods with million-dollar homes on every corner have to do with NASCAR?"

He spread his arms wide. "This is where two of NASCAR's newest drivers grew up, identical twins, Bart and Will Branch. While their childhoods may have been charmed and their NASCAR Nationwide Series careers filled with record wins, Will and Bart's current season has been anything but a cakewalk."

Neil spent several minutes panning across the tree-lined streets and perfectly manicured front lawns.

"That's good, Neil," Payton said. "Let's call it a day."

They'd spent the last two days interviewing Maeve and Penny Branch, Bart and Will's mother and older sister. While the Branch women had both been extremely photogenic, gracious to a fault and interesting enough to make the trip to Texas worth every minute of Payton's time, the staff at Maeve's club, where they'd done a good share of the filming, had been less than cooperative. This Dallas high-society crap was definitely not for Payton. He

was exhausted. Too bad they had an appointment to interview younger brother Sawyer Branch in the morning, or
he would've hightailed it back to Charlotte tonight.

"You hungry?" Neil asked, stowing his camera equipment in the trunk of their rental car.

Payton needed something substantial in his stomach.
"Let's get something at the hotel restaurant. I'm beat."
They climbed into the car and took off.

"Man, you're turning into a real deadbeat," Neil said,
turning onto the freeway.

"What do you mean?"

"We're in Dallas. Big city. Lots to do. Nightlife.
Women. Great food. And all you want to do is go back to
the hotel."

"Sorry. My back's killing me." That wasn't the whole
story and Neil knew it. Payton simply didn't have an
interest in going out. More than anything he wanted to
find out how Justin had done in today's race. Neil drove
to the hotel's front door and waited for Payton to hop out.

"Our appointment with Sawyer's at 9:00 a.m.," Payton
said, climbing out of the car. "So don't have too much fun."

"You're the one who has to be pretty for the camera.
Not me."

Payton bought a cold sandwich and headed to his
room. He lay down on the bed, took out his cell phone
and stared at it, debating. Could he call her? No. She'd
made things crystal clear as to where he didn't fit into her
life and where she expected to fit into his.

He flipped on the TV, went directly to the racing
channel, hoping for an update on the day's racing
results and wishing he'd skipped coming to Texas and
used his station budget to fly to New Hampshire. He

actually missed all the action, the heat, the crazy, excited fans, the smells of fuel and burning rubber. Go figure. Payton went still when the announcer mentioned Fulcrum.

"Today's results were a mixed bag for the Fulcrum team with Shakey Paulson coming in fifth and Justin Murphy finishing a disappointing eighteenth…"

Damn. That's when Payton realized he was hooked. On NASCAR. On Rachel. A big gaping hole had been sliced right out of his gut. He missed her, missed the woman who was becoming his best friend.

RACHEL WAS LATE.

That never happened, at least not to her, anyway.

The Fulcrum team had rented one of the local tracks near Concord for practice and while the rest of the guys had been out there testing a new car for the coming weekend's race, she'd been stuck in her office, clearing up some problems with one of their parts suppliers. She sped into the track parking lot and jumped out of her truck.

"How's the car doing?" she asked after joining Hugo on top of the hauler.

"See for yourself." Her uncle leaned against the metal rail, watching the track and chuckling to himself.

The No. 448 car weaved left and right as if the driver might be warming the tires, but that was like no motion she'd ever seen her brother make. She glanced trackside and saw Justin standing there, talking and laughing with the rest of the team.

So who was driving?

The weaving stopped and the car accelerated in earnest. Rachel's palms turned sweaty and she quickly scanned the group below. The entire Fulcrum team was trackside, watching.

"Hugo," she said, "who's in that car?"

"Heh, heh, heh." Hugo flipped back his cap and chuckled some more. "Who do you think?"

"Payton?" *Oh my God.* "Is Payton driving?"

Her uncle nodded. "And he's doing a pretty good job, first time or not."

"You okay'd this?"

"Justin's been after me ever since he saw that climbing documentary. Didn't take any convincing at all to get Payton behind the wheel. I do believe he started drooling the second your brother made the offer. Look at your boy go."

Whether she wanted to watch or not, Rachel couldn't take her eyes off the track. Payton's driving was a bit on the green side, but he was giving the track a good run. He accelerated and accelerated some more until he seemed to find a good pace.

"He found his groove," Hugo said.

After several more laps, he slowed and came to a stop in front of the team. Rachel's fear was quickly replaced by anger. At Hugo. At Justin. And definitely at Payton.

The average person had no concept of the kind of power under the hood of a stock car. At those speeds, if a tire had blown, Payton might have lost control, sideswiped the wall and rolled, or crashed head-on.

"I can't believe you let him do that." Pulling off her hat, she swatted her uncle on the shoulder.

Hugo raised his eyebrows at her before she climbed down from the hauler and headed trackside. By the time she joined the rest of the team, they were all patting Payton on the back and congratulating him. Proud of themselves, proud of him.

"Good run!"

"Mountain climber turns driver."

"Way to go, Payton."

"I'm impressed."

All that testosterone made her want to puke.

"You guys are all a bunch of idiots!" Rachel pushed her way into the group. She jabbed her brother in the chest. "And you're King Idiot."

"Rayray—"

"Don't Rayray me." She turned to Payton. God, it was good to see him again. "You told me you've never driven a race car before."

His triumphant smile faded. "I haven't."

"Then what do you think you're doing driving that fast?"

He was holding a helmet in one hand and driving gloves in another, and he looked awfully good in one of Justin's racing uniforms. "Rachel, I would never have wrecked your car."

"You think I care about that hunk of metal? Fulcrum goes through cars the way an average person goes through underwear."

Like a splash of water to a burning face, the anger fizzled and fear returned. Tears sprang from nowhere. Quickly, she lowered her head and stalked away, embarrassed at her emotional outburst. She was heading toward the parking lot when a hand landed on her shoulder.

"What?" She spun around, faced Payton and tried her best to bring back the anger she'd felt at the track.

"Me?" he asked. "You were worried about me?"

She couldn't say it. The words stuck in her throat, choking her. She usually didn't worry about Justin racing every week. He was a trained professional.

But Payton. She spun around again, not wanting him to see this terrible weakness.

"I'm sorry, Rachel." The softness in his voice undid her. This big, strong man could be so, so gentle. "Rachel?" He touched her shoulder.

Tears spilled onto her cheeks. "I missed you."

He came around and without a word folded her into his arms, kissed the top of her head. He felt so good. Rachel wished he would never let her go. But he would be letting her go. Soon.

She drew in a shaky breath. The new her, the one who was trying her darnedest to open up and let other people in, didn't want to lose another minute with Payton. "Can we go back to being friends?"

"I'll always be your friend. Nothing could ever change that."

But she had a feeling something already had changed. She was falling in love with her best friend.

"I DON'T COOK," Rachel said. "At all."

"Now, why does that not surprise me?" Payton poured a glass of cabernet and handed it to her. He figured the least he could do after scaring her half to death that morning was to make her a nice meal. "Sit down, relax and I'll cook for you."

She slipped into a chair at the countertop in her kitchen and watched him take things out of the paper bag. He knew from past experience that her kitchen was not well stocked, so along with several limes and mangos, new potatoes and asparagus, he'd purchased every major spice from A to Z.

"You needed something to put in all these nice, new cabinets." He stacked the bottles on a rack above the stove.

"Where did you learn to cook?"

"After Dad died, Mom went to work full-time. I was the oldest. After a while, we all got pretty sick of macaroni and cheese and frozen pizzas." He shrugged. "Good thing, too. 'Cause when you're out in the boonies, there's no Chinese takeout. It's amazing what you can accomplish when you're motivated."

"What are those?" She pointed to several ovalish, green, red-and-orange, rubbery-skinned fruits.

"Mangos." He unwrapped a white butcher's package and noticed Rachel grimacing.

"Payton, I hate to say this, but other than fried catfish, I'm not much for seafood."

"That's okay. Salmon's different from other fish. If you don't like it, there'll be plenty of other food." He proceeded to peel the mango and slice it away from the pit. "While you're sitting there, chop this for me." He handed her a cutting board, a knife and the bowl of large mango slices.

"Hey, I'm supposed to be relaxing."

He tossed the asparagus in the sink and rinsed it off. "Every cook needs a helper," he whispered. "You do this right and I'll have a few other things you can *help* me with after dinner."

"That sounds like a promise."

"It is." He turned on some music and set to work on the rest of the meal. It felt good to be back in her house. The place was almost finished.

In between sips of wine, she chopped, cleaned, sliced and squeezed whatever he put in front of her. He threw the salmon, marinated with lime and mango, on the grill and came back inside.

"I'm having a party next week to celebrate the house

being finished," she said. "Can you help me arrange furniture?"

"Sure."

"Will you come to the party?"

"Of course I'll come."

"Promise?"

"Promise."

They ate outside. It was hot, but her deck was shaded this time of day. He watched her tentatively poke at the pinkish hunk of salmon and pop a taste into her mouth.

"Don't make any big commitments there."

She tilted her head and chewed. "Hey, this salmon's pretty good."

"Thank you."

She was starving and proceeded to eat everything on her plate, one bite after another.

"The flowers look great." He pointed to the pots they'd planted several weeks earlier and couldn't believe that with her travel schedule they hadn't dried up and died. Then he remembered arguing, after planting them. The things that had been left unsaid sprung between them.

"There's a neighbor girl who brings in my mail and waters everything when I'm at the races."

"No kidding?"

She nodded. "I've introduced myself to several of the families who live on the other side of the orchards. I invited them all to the party," she said, pleased with herself.

He leaned back in his chair. "Rachel, does this party have anything to do with that day Kim went into the hospital?"

She nodded.

"Listen, I said some things—"

"That were very true."

"True or not, I didn't mean to hurt you. I'm sorry."

"Don't be. These changes are good for me." Rachel hopped up and grinned at him. "You cooked. I'll clean."

He followed her inside, carrying his empty plate and the other side dishes. She filled the sink with hot, soapy water. "Your turn to relax now," she said.

"Every cleaner needs a helper." He snuck behind her, wrapped his arms around her waist, and nuzzled his face in her hair. She smelled like fresh air with a hint of exhaust and all he could think about was how he didn't mind. At all.

"You keep doing that and we're gonna need a new cleaner."

He pressed his lips to her neck, moved his hands up her sides, and she let her head fall back against his chest.

She spun around in his arms. "Payton—"

"I don't want to talk anymore." He closed his mouth over hers, wanting a taste of her, and, instead, all he could sense was his own frustration. What the hell were they doing together? He wanted her. He shouldn't want her. She was his friend. He didn't want to be friends.

"I feel crazy." He grabbed her at the waist, set her on top of the counter and slid her toward him. "I don't know whether I'm coming or going. What we are, what we're not."

They met eye to eye, chest to chest. Rachel wrapped her legs around him and connected with him. A shudder ran through her and she pressed closer. "That makes two of us."

He could sleep with her and leave in the morning. He'd been doing exactly that with women for many years. He pressed against her and closed his eyes, felt her softness, wanted to take her right there, right then. "What if…friends isn't enough anymore?"

She hesitated, explaining her answer better than any words.

He bit back the words on the tip of his tongue. *I want you. You want me. One night, Rachel, that's all. Nobody will get hurt.* He stepped away, wanting something from her she'd made very clear she wasn't ready to give. She was trying to do the right thing. He wasn't.

"Payton? Are you okay?"

"No." He shook his head. "Did you know a man will say about anything to get what he wants?"

"Yeah. I know."

"I'm no different than the rest." He headed toward the door.

"So you're going to leave me in this mess?"

"I cooked. You clean. You'll thank me in the morning."

CHAPTER NINETEEN

"WHERE'S ALL THIS stuff supposed to go?" Justin lifted his hands out to his sides. He, Hugo, Loren, Fred and some other Fulcrum guys stood in Rachel's family room with a load full of new furniture and accessories she'd bought pushed up against one wall.

The party that had started out as a small get-together had quickly mushroomed into one of the biggest blowouts in recent Murphy history. Practically everyone Rachel knew or ever had known would be coming, including family, NASCAR crew and old friends, such as the Stroms. People she'd invited, but hardly met, neighbors and the rest of the construction crew, would probably come out of curiosity, if nothing else.

Rachel wanted her entire house as close to perfect as possible. All of her old stuff, things she'd purchased from garage sales and thrift stores after graduating from college, had looked ridiculous once all the renovations had been completed. The time for grown-up furnishings was long overdue.

So in one frenzied night, something Rachel had been saving the last ten years for, she and Kim had searched through several local stores and proceeded to outfit every room in her house. She'd had to push Kim in a wheelchair, but Rachel never could've finished such a job alone.

Overwhelmed now with the results, Rachel turned toward Kim. Hugo had told her crew chiefs had to learn how to delegate, right? "I need your help, Kim. What do you think?" She didn't want to address the small truckload of stuff still sitting out on the driveway.

Without moving from her countertop stool, Kim pointed. "Couch, love seat, chair, chair. TV over here. End table, end table, coffee table."

"Are you sure?" Rachel asked, thinking analytically. "That messes up the straight line to the bathroom."

The guys nodded.

Kim chuckled. "Do you want it to look nice or run like one of your engines?"

"All right." Rachel glanced at the guys. "What she said."

Hugo laughed. "You heard 'em, boys. Let's go."

While Kim directed, the men moved the larger stuff and Rachel set up the tables and lamps and hung family pictures and a few pieces of art. Justin took care of the TV, wiring the cables and components. Hugo and Loren hung a fancy new rod with simple yet colorful draperies around the large picture window that framed the front of the yard. The large floor-to-ceiling windows facing the lake remained, for a perfect view, unadorned.

A short while later, about when Rachel felt like tearing her hair out, a few of the men's wives appeared. Rachel had met all of them either at the race tracks or various Fulcrum events, but she'd never gotten to know them.

"We heard you might need some help," Molly, Fred's wife, said.

Loren's wife, Amy, smiled. "Tell us what you want us to do. We're all yours."

"I'm so glad you guys came." Rachel gave every one of them a hug, then she turned around and yelled for the manager. "Kim!"

Several hours later, the house looked spectacular, better than anything Rachel could have envisioned, let alone planned and executed. The pizzas Rachel had ordered were delivered and they all brought chairs into the backyard, along with a cooler full of beer, sodas and water. It was the end to an almost perfect day. Only one person had been missing, and she wasn't the only one who'd noticed.

"Where's Payton?" Dripping wet, Justin came from a dip in the lake and reached for one of the towels Rachel had brought outside.

"He's out of town." Avoiding her brother's inquisitive gaze, she handed another towel to Loren.

"Will he be back for the party?" Loren asked.

"He'll be here."

At least, Payton had said he'd be back in their last cryptic phone conversation. Rachel had no idea where or why he'd gone, and she didn't blame him for keeping his distance.

He'd been right, of course, that night he'd made dinner here at her house and left her sitting on the kitchen counter, hot and bothered. Well, he'd gotten part of it right, anyway. She'd have slept with him in a heartbeat. The part he'd gotten wrong was in believing that in the morning she'd have regretted their actions.

Pain was out there, waiting, threatening, a storm cloud hovering on her horizon. For the first time in her life, she felt ready for it, almost wanted it to come.

"YOU'RE AS HEALTHY as a horse, Payton." The doctor folded his hands over the files on his desk.

"There's nothing wrong with my heart?"

"You're the fittest thirty-two-year-old I've ever known."

"That doesn't answer my question." Payton folded his arms over his chest. For the last two days, he'd been examined, poked, prodded, hooked into monitors and practically drained of blood for all the tests the Mayo Clinic could possibly do in a complete, top-to-bottom workup. After all that, he wanted a straight answer to one simple question. "Is there anything wrong with my heart?"

"No." The doctor shook his head. "There is absolutely nothing wrong with your heart."

"How do you know?" Payton stood and paced the room. "People die after visiting doctors all the time. They get tests, have surgeries. How can you be so sure there's nothing wrong with me?"

The doctor narrowed his eyes. "Every year you come in here for the most thorough annual exam known to man. Every year I tell you the same thing. And every year you walk out of this room reassured that you'll live." The doctor leaned forward in his chair. "What's different this time, Payton?"

Payton had been coming to this doctor for the past ten years. He'd always felt fine, perfectly healthy, but he had the tests done anyway. If something was going to knock him down, he wanted to know what was coming. This year, though, he felt like crap, and for the first time ever he was actually worried.

"Something's wrong, Payton. What are you not telling me?"

He paced some more. "I'm not sleeping. I've lost my appetite. I can't concentrate."

The doctor glanced at a file. "You haven't lost any weight, and your BMI looks good. How's your job?"

"Great. Better than I'd ever planned."

"Could depression be a possibility?"

"Doubt it. All things considered, I'm a pretty happy guy."

"Still climbing?"

"Not much."

"You're still working out."

"Every day."

"Notice any allergies? North Carolina suit you?"

Better than Payton had expected. "No allergies."

"All of your health indicators are well within the normal ranges, Payton. And you know that." He sat back and sighed. "Why don't you quit worrying about dying and live a little?"

That stung, hit maybe too close to home. "Do you know what it feels like facing the possibility of being the oldest male in your family's history?"

"No."

"I've got two brothers, watching and waiting."

"Let's hope they're staying healthy while they're at it."

"They are." As far as Payton knew.

"I don't blame you for worrying, Payton. I really don't. But I've studied all the files, over and over again. Your family history. Your own health history. You are in perfect condition. You're doing everything right. Everything you possibly can." The doctor sighed again, heavily this time. "There's no reason to believe that you couldn't live to one hundred. It won't kill you to cut yourself some slack."

Easy for him to say.

"We've known each other a long time, been fairly open

all along." The doctor tapped a pencil on his desktop. "How's your sex life?"

Payton glared back at him.

The doctor chuckled. "Well, there you go."

HER STOMACH SLOWLY CHURNING, Rachel drove up alongside Harlan and Catie's modest split-level home on a quiet Mooresville street with mature trees and lots of shade. She did *not* want to do this. As if opening up to people wasn't new and awkward enough for her, teenagers were the worst. Time and time again, she'd seen them with Justin. He'd walk into a room and immediately all the sullen, disinterested faces turned expectant and needy.

Rachel was Catie's Justin.

What if Rachel let her down? Screwed up, said the wrong thing or, worst of all, couldn't fix the engine?

She glanced out her pickup's passenger window. A group of kids, boys and girls, hung out by the workbench inside Catie's garage, cans of energy drinks, sodas or water in their hands.

Great. Just great. It wasn't just one or two of them, it was a whole bunch of teenagers.

"Rachel!" Catie ran onto the driveway.

No turning back now.

Rachel parked and climbed out of her truck. She was disappointed to notice a spot of grease on her brown pants, and reminded herself this was a bunch of kids. Most likely they wouldn't care what she was wearing, how she looked. Most likely.

"Hey, Catie." A rock tune that Rachel was happy she recognized blared out the open garage door. A car, probably the one Catie had been restoring, sat in one of the garage bays with a dust cover over it.

"Thanks for coming." Catie grinned; her eyes danced.

"No problem. I hope I can help." She walked up the driveway and into the shade of the garage.

A skinny young man, barely taller than Catie, with curly, light brown hair walked toward Rachel.

"Rachel, this is my friend Derek. We've been working on the car together."

"Hi, Derek."

Catie's friend nodded. "Hi, Rachel."

"I hope you don't mind some of my other friends wanted to come by and meet you."

"Nope. That's fine." It was not fine, but Rachel was supposed to be the grown-up here.

Catie introduced the four boys and their girlfriends. Strange, the boys seemed tongue-tied, and the girls didn't seem to know what to do with themselves. If they didn't know, how the heck was Rachel supposed to help them out? One of the girls eyed her Fulcrum uniform with not quite obvious distaste, while another was clearly jealous of the respect and attention her boyfriend was paying Rachel.

"Could you sign this poster of Justin?" the boyfriend in question asked.

That was a first. "I'll do one better. You guys leave your names with Catie, and I'll make sure she gets an autographed poster of Justin for each of you." Her brother was the star, and that was more than fine with Rachel.

"Sweet!"

"Awesome!"

Catie smiled at Derek and then turned to Rachel,

suddenly so excited she was practically jumping out of her own skin. "You wanna see it?"

"Absolutely." Rachel put on her game face, preparing herself for a bad paint job, worse upholstery repairs or an engine that she might have to rebuild from scratch. If she had to, she'd already resolved to tow the poor thing into Fulcrum, whatever it would take to provide this young lady with a drivable vehicle by her sixteenth birthday.

Catie slipped off the cover.

Rachel couldn't have been more surprised. She stared at a paint finish that shone like glass on the two-door coupe. "Ooooh, baby." She couldn't help but whistle, long and low. "This is the nicest Chevelle I've seen in a long time."

Catie beamed, her eyes misted.

"Is it a '68?" Rachel knew it wasn't, but she couldn't resist pumping Catie. "Stock paint?"

"Seventy. Nope. I couldn't afford anything other than this color." An understated green with white stripes down the hood and trunk areas.

"Where'd you find her?"

"In my grandma's barn outside Kannapolis. She was rusting out and the engine hadn't been turned over for twenty years."

"She sure is pretty."

"Check out the interior." Derek opened the driver's-side door. "That alone took us over a month."

Dark green leather. "You two do all this yourself?"

She nodded. "We started it last summer."

While the other boys kept their attention on Rachel, it was clear Derek thought the sun rose and set on Catie. Catie didn't seem to notice.

"Looks to me as if you have it all under control."
Rachel shook her head. "What do you need me to do?"

"She won't start."

Rachel popped the hood. V8, 350 horsepower. Pretty
engine and one of the most powerful muscle cars ever
built. Zero to sixty in sixty seconds. "Did you guys
rebuild this yourself?"

She and Derek both nodded. "We've gone over it a
hundred times and still can't figure out what's wrong."

From what she'd seen so far, Rachel figured it was fair
to assume they'd done their homework with the engine
itself. She checked out all the wiring and cable hookups.
The battery was new. Without bringing it into the garage,
she was afraid she might not be able to resolve this for
Catie. "Can I try to start it? See if I can hear anything?"

"Sure," Catie said.

"Go for it." Derek tossed her the keys.

Rachel slid inside and tried turning it over. Churn,
churn, churn. The engine was moving all right, but it
wasn't firing. "I know this is going to sound silly, but did
you give her some gas?"

Catie glanced at Derek, his mouth dropped open and
they both laughed. "Oh my God! I can't believe we forgot
something so simple." She ran over to a gas can on the
shelf above the lawn mower.

"Normally, you'd use premium in that engine."

"I know," Catie said, "but this'll work to get started,
right?"

Rachel nodded. "Use only enough to get her to a gas
station." She was about to tell her to put some gas in the
distributor when Catie took care of it. This kid knew what
she was doing.

Catie emerged from under the hood. "Try it again, Rachel."

"Oh, no." Rachel slid out and handed the keys back to Catie. "This is your moment."

Catie climbed in, shared a look with Derek and turned the key. The engine turned and turned. When it finally fired, it sounded like it might explode. The kids jumped back. Catie switched it off.

"Turn it on again."

"I don't wanna blow it up," Catie said, worried.

Rachel smiled. "You won't. Turn it on and listen. See if you can hear what's wrong."

Catie turned the key. "Is something wrong with the distributor?"

Rachel nodded. The engine wasn't firing in the right sequence. "See if you can figure it out." They'd come so far on their own. It'd be a shame for Rachel to take away their glory on the home stretch.

"The cylinders are firing in the wrong sequence," Derek said.

Catie turned off the engine and hopped out. She and Derek examined the distributor and talked back and forth about what the problem could be. "We could have it off 180 degrees."

Derek shrugged. "Let's give it a shot." He threw Catie a wrench.

She removed the bolts, turned the distributor and secured it back down. "Now try it."

Derek climbed inside and turned the key. The engine purred like a very loud cat with a cold, but it sounded a hell of a lot better than before. "Yes!" Derek jumped out and Catie ran to him. He picked her up and spun her around.

"We did it," she cried.

The other kids piled into the backseat of the Chevelle, all ready for a ride.

"Rachel, will you go out on the road with us?" Catie asked.

They were both fifteen with only learner's permits and needed adults in the car while driving. "I think you should wait for your daddy, Catie. He's going to be awfully proud."

"I'm not too sure about that." Catie's smile disappeared.

"I am." Catie didn't know it, but that car was worth a pretty penny.

"Rachel, thanks for your help. I can't believe we were so lame."

"Don't say that. Look at what you two did. She's a beauty." Rachel had to admit that hadn't been so bad. She pulled out a business card and handed it to Catie. "Call me anytime. Bring her into the Fulcrum shop when you get a chance and we'll get her tuned up. For now, I gotta run." Rachel headed toward her truck.

Catie and Derek followed her.

"Hey, Catie, when you're ready for a job, give me or Hugo a call."

"Do you mean that? Honestly?"

"Absolutely. You, too, Derek."

Rachel started her pickup and Derek leaned into the open passenger window. "We could use your help in shop class next year. Our teacher's great with woodworking but he doesn't know jack about engines."

Rachel instinctively recoiled at the thought of standing, front and center, in a roomful of students.

"His dad's the teacher." Catie good-naturedly pushed

at Derek's shoulder, making room for herself in Rachel's window. "We could definitely use your help."

"Definitely." Derek nodded.

Rachel studied their young faces and found a few of her own insecurities reflected back. She could do it. "After Homestead, when the season's over, have your dad give me a call. I'd be glad to help out up at your school."

CHAPTER TWENTY

PAYTON DROVE TO Rachel's house, turned off his engine and sat there, glancing at the cars and trucks already parked and lining the long drive. When she pulled out all the stops, she pulled them out but good.

Still, something about today's setup bothered him. Something that said *Payton, Rachel's boyfriend. Payton, the guy she's serious about. Not Payton, friend. Or Payton, the sportscaster who'll be moving to L.A. soon and hightailing it out of Rachel's life.*

His Branch family special had aired last weekend, and after NSN had picked it up they'd begun contract talks with his agent. Payton's ultimate goal had never been more clearly within his sights. Predictably, the urge to head out of there nipped at his heels. He turned the ignition key and fired the engine.

Payton, friend.

He rested his arms on the steering wheel. This feeling Rachel needed him here for some crazy reason troubled the far reaches of his conscience. He'd never been stellar at the friend thing, but, one thing was for sure, friends didn't blow off other friends.

Turning off the car and pocketing his keys, he walked across the yard and onto the porch, admiring the way the yellows, whites and pinks of the flowers brightened things. Her place looked homey, well loved and lived-in.

The heavy, antique door was wide-open and sounds of talking and laughter, a summer afternoon party, filtered through the screen door. A silhouette passed through the kitchen and at least one head was visible over the top of a chair on the deck.

"Hello. Anyone there?"

A shape, backlit from the lakeside windows of the house, appeared from the kitchen. "Payton. Come on in." It was Hugo.

He took a deep breath and stepped inside. Everything looked great, fully arranged with furniture, pictures, silk plants and other accessories. There wasn't a tool or speck of sawdust in sight. Oddly enough, he felt left out, wished he'd been here to help. "You guys did good."

"Thanks. We had quite a crew pitching in."

"Sorry. I was out of town."

Hugo shrugged. "Want a beer? You're not into those mojitos or anything fancy, are ya? She's got some of those in a pitcher on the deck. Along with waters and sodas. Watch out for that sweet tea though, it's packin' a punch."

"Beer's good."

"Keg's out back, but this is a fresh one. Take it. I better eat somethin' or I'll be taking a nap in that hammock she strung up by the lake." He held out a cold plastic cup with a nice foamy beer head.

"Thanks."

"You okay? You're kinda pale."

He didn't feel too good. "I'm fine. Queasy stomach is all."

"Everyone's out back. I was sent in on a mission to find some more paper plates and napkins."

"They're in the pantry. Over there." Before he could stop himself, Payton flicked his chin toward the tall cabinet next to the refrigerator.

Hugo grinned. "Thanks."

Payton had to get out of there. He crossed to the sliding screen door and found Kim, very thin and slightly pale, sitting in one of the patio chairs. He went onto the deck and squinted at the bright sunshine.

"Hi, Payton," she said. "You probably don't remember me. I'm Kim, Rachel's cousin."

"Sure, I remember you. Darlington. I was in pretty bad shape, though. Thanks for your help." After what she'd been through, she appeared on the mend. "And, no, you're not chopped liver."

She laughed while studying him. Although there was nothing judgmental in her gaze, she was clearly intrigued by his presence and sizing him up.

Don't bother, he wanted to say. *Friends.* Just friends.

"Rachel had so much fun rock climbing with you at Crowders Mountain. I couldn't get a word in edgewise when she was describing it to me. Your background sounds fascinating."

"Sounds more interesting than it really is." He leaned against the deck rail for a view of the activity in the backyard. He spotted Rachel's auburn hair immediately. She was laying out a slip-and-slide water toy thing for some young kids and, dressed in swimsuits, they were jumping up and down next to her.

She was a sight for sore eyes, sunlight dancing off her hair, a smile as wide as Half Dome on her face. If only he could walk down there, wish this party gone and make love to her in the grass. While that might solve one of his particular issues, it'd create a whole new set of problems.

He forced his gaze away from Rachel and spotted some guys from Fulcrum playing volleyball with several women, probably wives or girlfriends. The older kids hung out down by the dock at the water's edge. Rachel had rented a large party tent, but Payton had never met many of the folks sitting in the shade at the banquet tables.

Below the deck, on the patio, Justin was cooking shrimp and some kind of fish on the grill and a woman with light brown hair stood next to him, laughing. She was so out of place, he almost didn't recognize her. "Sophia Grosso's here?"

"Amazing, isn't it?" Kim sipped on some water. "It's an adjustment for Hugo and Rachel."

"You?" He glanced back at Kim.

"Not so much. Life's short, you know?" Her expression turned worried.

Yeah, he knew. Kim's kidney disease had to have impacted everyone. "How are you feeling these days?"

"Dialysis sucks, but I'm doing okay." She smiled ruefully. "Got a kidney you don't need?"

"I'll let you know." He smiled. "Do they have you on a list for a transplant?"

Kim nodded. "Though they've warned me a match will be difficult. I have a rare blood type."

Hugo came out of the house with a stack of paper supplies and proceeded down the steps to the patio. Amazingly, he seemed content with Sophia's presence.

Kim took a deep breath. "So now let's talk about you."

Here we go. Initial interrogation.

She proceeded to ask him questions about where he'd been, what climbs he'd done and so forth, with the occasional and quietly thrown-in curiosity about his future plans. She wanted to know his intentions toward Rachel, and he couldn't blame her.

When he got to the part about moving to L.A. and planning on documenting expeditions around the world, her eyes turned guarded. She was figuring, questioning, calculating.

"I love to hike, but I couldn't imagine doing all that," she said. "Especially not now."

"Payton!" Rachel climbed the deck stairs. She made a move as if to hug him, and then faltered, unsure.

He didn't want to make it easy for her. He was acting like an ass, and he knew it, but he wasn't sure why.

"When did you get here?"

"A few minutes ago."

"He's been keeping me company," Kim said.

"You're just in time to eat." She turned to Kim. "Do you need some help down the steps?"

"Oh, Rachel, I do declare I'm feeling faint." She put the back of her hand to her forehead and exaggerated her accent. "Payton, could you carry me?"

"Why of course, Miss Kim."

"Okay, okay, I get the hint." Rachel chuckled and held her hand out to stop Payton. "Don't even think about carrying her."

Payton shrugged. "I don't think I could if I wanted to."

"Sorry, Payton." Kim grinned. "My family's gotten overprotective of late, so I occasionally have to put them in their place."

He well remembered the suffocating feeling of family

hovering, especially his mother. For the first month, he'd barely been able to sit. Two months of physical therapy and six months of doctor appointments and he wasn't sure he'd ever be able to see any of his family again. Or, more aptly, whether his mom wanted to see *him* again.

"Come on. Let's eat." Rachel waved her hand toward the patio.

He followed Kim down the steps, greeted Justin and the rest of the team and suffered through introductions to wives, girlfriends and children. Even Harlan Strom, his daughter and several of his construction crew were there. Surprisingly, Rachel seemed relaxed.

If Payton had any doubts as to what people thought of his relationship with Rachel, they completely dissipated after seeing the seat next to her had been left open. For him. By the time he sat down, he wasn't sure he'd be able to force any food down his throat. He put a few things on his plate, some catfish, watermelon and some corn, but everything tasted like paste in his mouth.

Rachel leaned toward him and whispered, "You okay?"

"Stomach's bothering me." That, at least, was the truth. No point in telling her the rest, that all this touchy-feely togetherness of her family and friends made him want to pack his bags and drive as fast and as far away as he could get.

Snippets of conversations swirled around him.

"Remember that wedding…"

"…have to have this recipe…"

"While you're up, get me…"

"Hell, no! Bart Branch is not…"

"…such a pretty yard…"

Everyone else seemed perfectly happy. That's what got

him. Faces laughing, smiling, talking. Hugo was carrying on a conversation with Sophia Grosso. It was all genuine and comfortable, for them, anyway.

For the first time, it occurred to him that maybe he'd been wrong. Maybe Rachel wasn't the one who was stagnating. Maybe it was him. He was wrong for her. Rachel had a full and rich life here. She didn't need to run around the world with or without him searching for anything. She had it all right here.

And he didn't fit into *here*.

He'd known it, deep down inside, but it had never been so blatantly apparent to him as it was right now. He didn't fit into her life. Maybe as a friend, but friend wasn't enough anymore. He had to quit seeing her. For all their pretenses at being friends, they'd come to mean so much more to each other. *He* wanted more from her. Much more. But the closer she got to him, the more his leaving would hurt her.

"I gotta go," he whispered.

"Now?"

He pushed back his chair and stood. Everyone glanced over at him and grew quiet. "Sorry folks. I'm really not feeling well." He headed toward the side of the house.

Hugo looked concerned. "Take care of yourself, okay?"

"Get better," a few others offered.

Kim watched him, frowning.

"Come back later, Payton," Justin yelled. "We'll be here a while."

Rachel came up beside him. "What's going on?"

He didn't stop to answer her until he got to the front of the house, out of earshot of the party. "I was wrong."

"About what?"

"You and your family. They're great. They're perfect. You have a right to be happy with them."

"Payton—"

"I don't belong here, Rachel." He headed toward his car. "And we both know it."

"What are you talking about?"

"The way Kim looked at me, okay? She thinks I'm special. I'm not another guy friend in your life. I'm *him*. The one."

"No one ever said that."

"They don't have to. I can see it on all their faces."

"I don't care—"

"Rachel." He held her gaze. "I can see it on *your* face."

She didn't say anything. And all he wanted to do was hold her, tell her they'd make it work. Somehow. Some way. He shoved his hands through his hair. "I don't want to be just your friend anymore."

"Maybe I'm ready to be more than friends."

"No," he said, shaking his head. "You're not."

She reached for him. "Payton—"

He stepped out of her range. "NSN picked up my Branch special. They're talking contract with my agent. Right now."

"That's good. That's what you wanted."

"Rachel, wake up." He stepped back. "It won't be today. It might not be tomorrow, but it'll happen. I guarantee it. I'll be leaving. I'll leave this place, NASCAR. You." He climbed in his car. "Hell, for that matter, I'm already half gone."

"YOU SURE YOU DON'T want help with the rest?" Hugo stood by Rachel's front door, his car keys in his hand.

"Positive. You guys did enough already," Rachel said. The leftover food from the party had all either been put away or divided among the straggling guests and everything outside had been picked up or thrown away. She wished Payton were still here, but her family couldn't help with that. "The rest of this mess can wait until morning."

"Night, Rachel." Her brother patted her on the back. "I had a great time today," he said through a yawn.

"Thanks for all your help." She stood back and smiled at Sophia. Better late than never. "I'm glad you came."

"It was a fun party," Sophia said. "Thanks for inviting me." Arm in arm, she and Justin disappeared into the night.

"Come on, Kim." Hugo headed off down the porch. "I'll give you a ride home."

Kim hugged Rachel. "Call me, okay?"

"Okay." But Rachel wasn't sure if she could.

Kim may have noticed something strange about Payton's disappearance, but there was nothing for her to say, nothing for her to do. Besides, Kim needed to focus on getting better. What was happening between Rachel and Payton was new territory, something Rachel didn't want to talk about. Something she was going to have to work out on her own.

She closed the front door, leaned back against the hard wood and glanced around her house. Everything had come together in the end. The furniture. The colors. The comfort. The way the rooms felt. Everything that reminded her of her parents was completely gone. It felt like her house now. It *was* her house. Today was the beginning of a time for new memories. Good ones with friends and family.

She walked through her family room and kitchen,

passed by the mess of half-empty cups of beer, open soda cans and paper plates, and went onto her deck. The colors in all the flowerpots greeted her like warm sunshine. Rachel couldn't look at them without smiling and thinking of Payton.

A cool breeze ruffled her hair. The moon sparkled off the surface of the water and cut a path across her backyard. It was a perfect summer night, the kind that made you want to sit by the water and curl your toes into the sand. The kind that made Rachel want to skinny-dip.

If Payton were here, maybe they would have.

Walking down to the water's edge, she sat down in the swing. A hazy vision of her mother's profile lingered at the edges of her memory, her mother's long hair shifting in the breezes down by the water's edge.

This was why she was here.

Payton would leave. She was sure of that. But Rachel would still have the lake, this house, her new friends. A life. No one could take all that away from her.

PAYTON TURNED THE KEY on his apartment door and stepped inside. A cold, air-conditioned blast hit the sweat on his skin, immediately cooling him. He was exhausted, could barely move his legs. If a fifteen-mile run couldn't douse the fire in him, nothing would.

He slowly walked into his kitchen and drank a full glass of water. An odd sense of disappointment settled in his gut. Nothing in this room, other than a few dirty dishes in the sink, indicated he'd entered the correct apartment. In the main living area, a black leather couch sat in front of a large, flat-panel TV. Those, he knew, were his.

Making his way toward his bedroom, where a bed and a side table were the room's only furnishings, he threw his keys onto the black quilt and plopped down on the edge of the king-size mattress and closed his eyes.

Home sweet home.

What did that mean?

The image that came to mind wasn't this bare-bones apartment, or any of the number of apartments he'd rented through the years. He didn't envision the house in which he'd grown up in San Francisco. Instead, he couldn't get Rachel's place out of his mind. The smell of the lake, the feel of the soft breeze coming in off the water. The sound of people laughing and having a good time. The feel of her snuggled under his arm.

He was a mess.

For the first time in his life, his plans seemed to be falling apart. He didn't know where he was going, or why. He put his head in his hands and before he could give himself a moment to think about it, grabbed the phone and dialed. He waited, listening to the ringing.

"Hello." She sounded the same.

Emotion tickled the back of his throat. At least something was still right in this world.

"Is anyone there?"

"Hi, Mom."

"Payton! Are you all right?"

"Yeah, I'm fine. Is it too late to call?"

"Good heavens, no. You sure you're okay?"

"Honest. I just wanted to talk." Apparently Payton wasn't as accepting of losing track of his family as he'd previously believed. "I've missed you," he said. "And I didn't even know it…"

CHAPTER TWENTY-ONE

"COME ON, DADDY. Will you go for a ride now?"

Harlan tossed his truck keys onto the kitchen counter-top and stretched out his neck. It had been a tough day, worse than most Fridays. Between the clients complaining about something not being done right and subcontractors complaining about not having enough time to complete jobs, he'd been ready to tear out what little hair he had left.

"She's all tuned up," Derek said.

"You promised," Catie pleaded. "Please."

She turned sixteen in a few days, and he realized then she wouldn't need him anymore. This might be the last time she ever asked him to ride with her anywhere. Besides, when had he ever been able to turn down that pretty face? "Okay. Let's go."

Both kids practically ran out into the garage and that childish impulse coming from two tough teenagers put a smile on Harlan's face, first one all day.

Catie climbed behind the wheel.

"Mr. Strom, you take shotgun," Derek said. "I'll sit in the back."

"Listen to this, Daddy." She fired her up. "After we got done tuning it, Rachel said she's never heard a prettier-sounding engine."

Harlan listened. Miracles never ceased. "You sure did smooth her out."

"Rachel gave me her cell number. She said to call her anytime if I need to use Fulcrum's tuner. If me and Derek work on another car, she might help."

There was hope for Rachel yet. That'd put a smile on Hugo's face.

Catie backed out of the drive and turned onto their street. "Where should we go?"

"I'm hungry for some dinner," Harlan said. "Isn't there a drive-in toward the lake?"

As they headed through town, Harlan began feeling a bit like royalty. Guys in fancy, expensive cars looked over at Catie's Chevelle and nodded in appreciation. A couple of them even honked.

They pulled into the drive-in and decided to sit at a picnic table to eat their burgers, onion rings and fries. Everyone admired Catie's car as they walked by. As they were finishing eating, a guy about Harlan's age stopped and walked around Catie's car. He glanced back at them. "This is your car," he said to Harlan.

Harlan nodded at Catie. "My daughter's."

Catie's eyes sparkled.

"Who did the work?"

"We did," Catie said, motioning toward Derek. The three of them threw away their trash and walked back to the car.

"This is the nicest Chevelle I've seen in a long time. How's she running?"

"Like a kitten. Wanna hear?" With a grin, she climbed inside and turned her over.

"Would you mind popping the hood?"

Catie was proud to, and while the guy looked around

she and Derek explained where they'd gotten the parts and any problems they'd encountered. After a few minutes, the guy closed the hood. "Would you be willing to sell her?"

"No." Catie shook her head.

"I'll give you forty thousand."

Harlan choked on his root beer. "Dollars?" *Hells bells.*

The man nodded. "I ain't offering you pennies, that's for sure."

Catie and Derek hooted to high heaven and jumped into each other's arms. Harlan wasn't sure what he was more shocked about, the price tag on that Chevelle or the fact that Derek looked like he might kiss Catie. And Catie looked like she might kiss him right back.

Harlan scratched his head. "You serious?"

"Yes, sir. I'm opening a classics dealership next month over by the highway, and this Chevelle would be a mighty fine centerpiece."

"Catie?" Harlan said. "What do you think? That's a lot of money."

She and Derek had pulled away, but Harlan noticed they were still holding hands. They glanced sideways at each other and said, practically in unison, "She's not for sale."

Pride swelled in Harlan's chest. And relief. Catie was going to be okay.

"But we'll build you another one." She slipped her arm around Derek's waist.

The man nodded. "That's a deal."

PAYTON HADN'T WANTED to come here tonight, but Jay hadn't given him a choice. He sat motionless behind the wheel of his car in Rachel's driveway, knowing she had to be having a tough week. The No. 448 car had run out of gas at last Sunday's race in Daytona, and that could signify more engine issues for her to battle.

A sky full of clouds dimmed the fading sunlight, making the time seem later than it was. Faint light from Rachel's kitchen spilled through the window into the grass, but there didn't seem to be any movement in the entire house. Because he couldn't see her didn't mean she wasn't there.

He could feel her. Almost smell her.

"Payton?" Rachel came from the side of the house, a lawn and leaf bag in one hand. She must have been in the back doing yard work. She hoisted the bag into the Dumpster and walked to his car. "What are you doing here?"

She seemed distant. Heck, he wouldn't blame her if she'd been downright angry. What could he possibly say this time to put things right between them? What would be the point?

"I need your approval, preferably tonight." He picked up the DVD from the passenger car seat and held it out between them.

"What's that?"

"*On the Road,* the Murphys."

"You finished our family?"

"Yep."

She looked at the DVD, then back at him. Anger, hurt, uncertainty all passed over her features. She seemed to master each emotion in turn.

"I don't want to hurt you, Rachel."

"I know."

"Call me." He pushed the DVD toward her. "Let me know what changes you want made."

"Stay. Watch it with me?"

He should. It was his job.

"Please."

He owed her this, at least. "Okay."

She took the plastic case out of his hand and ran into her house. He followed, more slowly, found her already sitting down in her family room, the big-screen TV on and the remote in her hand. "Keep an open mind, all right?"

"No, sirree." Rachel grimaced at him, his transgressions forgotten. "You promised you'd take out anything I don't like."

"And I will. Don't worry. I'm just asking you to watch the whole thing before you come to any conclusions." Unaccountably nervous, he sat down in one of her new chairs, wanting—needing—to keep his distance. Carefully, he angled himself such that he could watch her reaction.

First the intro, the rock music WJAZ had specifically produced for his *On the Road,* show blared through the room as snippets of NASCAR track footage, drivers, cars, and team members flashed over the screen. He'd always liked what they'd put together to promote him and his show. The station manager really got Payton, and what he was trying to put together. Something edgy and geared toward the younger generation of NASCAR fans.

Rachel didn't look impressed. "Did you do that intro?" she asked, pausing the show.

"My producer took care of it. Why?"

"As usual, it's Grossos, Grossos, Grossos." She shook her head, disgusted. "Their family is two drivers and a spotter to our family's one driver, crew chief, engine specialist and spotter, but that intro has at least three times the images of the Grosso family's cars, drivers and teams."

"You've got a good point. I'll fix it."

She sat back and resumed the show, the scowl on her face telling him she was expecting the worst.

"The name of Connor Murphy has been associated with racing almost since before NASCAR came into being." Payton's voice came through the speakers and echoed strangely though the room as old footage of Troy, Hugo and stock-car racing's beginnings flashed up on the screen. "Alongside all the famous names of NASCAR, the Murphys have historically been a part of the very framework of racing...."

Payton watched Rachel's face as he touched on her family's sad past. In covering the Murphys properly, he'd had to talk about the tragedy of her mother's suicide and her father's hit-and-run, so he'd been as brief and unbiased as possible.

"While Troy Murphy's death has been mired in rumor and speculation, his younger brother, Hugo, carried on the family racing traditions, becoming one of the most well-respected crew chiefs in NASCAR history."

The TV screen filled with current footage of Hugo sitting atop the war wagon at Richmond. Payton had hoped he'd captured Hugo's essence. More important, he'd hoped Rachel was happy with it. With dark glasses, headset and a grim expression, Hugo seemed serious and intimidating. There was even a shot from last weekend of him yelling at one of the pit crew when they'd run out of gas and finished so badly. There was no doubt the older Murphy expected excellence from his team.

But Payton managed to capture Hugo before several races joking with the team and celebrating after the win in Atlanta, and his jovial side became immediately apparent.

When the clips of Hugo with Kim appeared, Rachel smiled for the first time. Then there were several of him with Rachel and Justin at various tracks. Though never typically demonstrative, it was clear from the angle of Hugo's head to the penetration of his gaze that the man adored his family. His feelings of affection and protectiveness were unmistakable.

"How did you get that footage? I don't remember seeing you."

"Watched and waited." Once he'd decided to do some of the filming himself, things had gotten interesting.

"Those are nice," Rachel murmured, not taking her eyes off the screen. "But Kim looks tired."

He'd included a brief blurb about Kim living near Charlotte and working as a research scientist before he turned to Justin. While he'd focused on Justin's record of wins, Payton had been honest about his reputation for partying and causing track pileups. Some of it was true. Some of it wasn't. Next came a shot of Justin with Sophia Grosso, and Rachel's lips momentarily flattened.

"Some speculate his recent engagement could put Justin on the straightway to a Cup victory, but who will Sophia root for, her dad, her brother or her fiancé?"

"I'm a lucky driver." Justin's voice sounded about the room. "Having my sister working on my engines, I know I'm in good hands." His laughter filled the room and Rachel's smile softened. "'Course, I'm awfully careful to stay on her good side."

A picture of Rachel from their first meeting at Richmond flashed onto the wide-screen TV. She was coming out from under the hood of the No. 448 car, obviously irritated.

Payton watched her reaction.

"I thought you were the biggest ass." She chuckled. "Can't believe you put that in there."

Images of her in the garages, tools in hand and working on engines, and in the pits at various tracks, in sunglasses and a headset, depicted her as serious about cars and racing. He'd included one of many clips of her, Hugo and Wade talking about adjustments to the No. 448 car. The men had gone with her suggestion to tighten the springs.

He'd wanted to show the world that this woman lived and breathed NASCAR and should be respected for her knowledge and dedication. Yet she hadn't lost her femininity. He'd caught her taking off her hat and shaking loose her full head of hair. It had been an unconsciously seductive motion, one that had shown her softer side.

"Where was that?"

"Dover," he whispered. "This next shot, I didn't know the camera was on. I swear."

It was a close-up of Rachel's face, freckles and the green in her hazel eyes shining. She looked up at something. It was so…Rachel. Honest, sweet, friendly, not the guarded and analytical technician she projected to the rest of the world. She'd shown herself to Payton in that private moment in Pocono. He'd hugged her, and the smile she'd given him had been meant only for him. Still, he'd had to put the clip in. He wanted the rest of the world to know and love…his Rachel. The woman, if he was honest with himself, he was falling in love with.

He swallowed, felt his throat tighten.

"You really didn't know the camera was on?"

"Really."

Her face turned serious when the last shot popped up

on the screen. It was the scene where Payton had grabbed the camera out of Neil's hands and caught the four Murphys crossing the Michigan infield. That moment, more than any other, epitomized what the Murphys represented, a family who, despite a tragic past, was intensely devoted to one another. And to NASCAR.

The screen went blank, and the family room of Rachel's house turned quiet. He held his breath, waiting, unaware until that moment how much her opinion of his work mattered to him. He wasn't sure he cared anymore about ratings, or contract offers from NSN. He wanted Rachel to like it.

She finally turned to him with tears in her eyes. "Payton," she said, sucking in a trembling breath and barely containing her emotions, "thank you. That was the nicest tribute to the Murphy family anyone ever could have done."

He barely checked himself from brushing the tears from her cheeks. For her sake and for his, he had to distance himself. "It'll be airing this weekend." He stood and headed for the front door. "You can keep the DVD."

CHAPTER TWENTY-TWO

SIX MILES. And Payton still hadn't run Rachel out of his system. He picked up the pace. Six and a half miles. Seven.

Alone in the gym facility at his apartment building, he'd turned off both TVs—TVs that had been set to NSN. He increased the volume on his headset and let the music distract him from the fact that it was race time in Chicago.

Ten miles and his heart rate had been steady for several minutes. Enough of that. Time for more pull-ups. That'd take care of her.

He hopped off the treadmill, took a long drink from his water bottle, wiped the sweat from his hands and face and made his way to the machines. He looped fifty pounds of weights onto a dip belt and strapped the belt around his waist, reached for the bar, and did three sets of fifteen.

The last five were the hardest, but he needed this. Head to toe, complete body burnout. It'd been a while. And he had to do something to get his mind—and body—off thoughts of Rachel.

After taking off the weights, he did three more sets of behind-the-neck pull-ups. Done. Now for the hardest of all, one-armed babies. Right side. One. Two. Three. Barely. Left side. Ripped off three.

The last one about killed him, and he couldn't help but

feel let down. During his prime climbing days he would've managed hundred-pound weights, five one-armed pull-ups per side and topped it all off with a set of muscle-ups.

Rachel.

Maybe he could flip the nearest TV on for a minute or two and see how Justin was doing. A few minutes wouldn't hurt anything.

No. No. No.

More water. He went to the treadmill and interval trained, speeding up and slowing down depending on his heart rate. After five more miles, he was ready for abdominals. He lay back on a mat and did three sets of bicycles, and then three sets of extremely slow crunches. He rolled over onto his stomach and pushed off from the floor from his elbows and held himself in the plank pose for a count of fifty. Four more times. Done.

He collapsed onto the mat. That was it. He wasn't sure he could move his pinky. After lying there for a few minutes, he shifted into a sitting position. His hand shook as he brought the water bottle to his mouth and guzzled what was left. A long, slow breath, and he closed his eyes and listened to his heart. Strong, steady beats. Maybe the doctor was right. Maybe it was time to stop berating himself.

Easy for him to say.

Payton went through a series of stretches. He'd learned the hard way that he couldn't skip this part. The last time he tried, he'd woken up the next day and couldn't get out of bed; his leg had cramped, which in turn strained his back. It was the only way to keep his back limber, and he'd learned to almost enjoy this part.

Rachel.

Guess it was time for a few pushups. One. Two. He collapsed, couldn't do them.

Rachel.

Dammit. He flicked on the TV and listened to the commentators.

"...this isn't Shakey's best track."

"That's a fact, but his teammate is having a good run today. The No. 448 car's moved from starting position of tenth into third."

Payton breathed a sigh of relief. Justin was doing okay.

"Hold on now. We may have spoken too soon. Justin Murphy's having some trouble."

"He sure is. Falling back pretty fast. He's smoking."

"Watch out! The No. 448 car blew an engine!"

"Oh, no." Payton shook his head, turned up the TV volume.

"Look at all that smoke. The cars behind Justin Murphy better watch out. He better get off the track before he gets T-boned."

"He's limping back to the garage."

"Can they put a new engine in? Or is he done for the day?"

"Takes too long for a new engine."

"Dammit!" Payton threw his water bottle.

"*Justin Murphy's out of the race.*"

"A VALVE," Rachel said. "That's the only problem I found when I disassembled the engine."

"What kind of valve?" Hugo asked from where he sat at the head of the long conference table.

"Air suction," she said, turning to look at each man in

the room. "It looks as if the valve got stuck open, so when Justin decelerated—"

"The airflow admitted caused an afterburn," Wade finished for her.

"Exactly." Rachel nodded.

"So it wasn't the tires," Justin said. "And it didn't have anything to do with the car being loose. It was the damned engine. Again." He stood and stared down Johnny Meline as he paced the conference room. "First, unknown engine problems. Then I run out of gas. And now I blow an engine—"

"The engines are fine here at the shop," Meline interrupted, looking right at Rachel. "I'm not sure what happens after they leave here."

Rachel bit the inside of her cheek to keep from screaming her frustrations at the top of her lungs.

"Hold on now." Hugo put out his hands, quieting the room. "Was the valve faulty in any way?" he asked Rachel.

"Probably," Meline said.

"Rachel, what do you think?"

"Everything was fried pretty good. I'm sorry. I couldn't tell. All I know is it was open."

"What do you *think* happened?"

The room grew quiet as all eyes settled on her. Rachel hesitated, tapping her toes on the carpet and bouncing her knee. If she didn't say what'd been on her mind for the past months, get it out in the open, this entire season might be a bust. If she did say what she was really thinking, Meline would jump down her throat.

She looked to Justin. Then Hugo. They actually needed her. She had to stand up to Meline. Right here. Right now.

After a deep breath, she blurted out in one long stream,

"I know it sounds simple, but I think it's the exhaust system. It's what I've been saying since way back in Richmond. The air's not flowing right with the new COT design. Airflow backed up. Pushed the valve open—"

"That's a bunch of crap," Meline interjected.

Hugo put out a hand, silencing Meline. "Rachel, we've spent hours with the COT in the wind tunnel. And on computer simulations. It didn't appear as if the exhaust system was affected that dramatically."

"That's because it isn't," Meline jumped in again. "That's what I've been telling her."

Hugo held out his hand and kept his gaze on Rachel. "Explain."

"I know this sounds strange, and I don't know if I can explain it. It's more an engineering gut feel."

"This has nothing to do with airflow," Meline said, preempting. "I went through the Chicago logs. The adjustments at the track are the problem. Tire pressure up and down. Wedges in and out. Guesses. One after another. There's no room for guessing in this business." He stared right at her. "If you're not careful, Rachel, one of your *guesses* might cost us the championship."

Rachel felt her skin turn hot and then cold. Angry adrenaline shot through her system, making her hands shake. For Meline to suggest she was jeopardizing their team's performance was tantamount to a punch in the gut. It was everything she could do to keep from outright punching Meline.

Justin leaned in. "Meline, you better watch your mouth."

But the noxious seed had been planted.

Hugo scratched the back of his neck and took a deep breath. Her own uncle didn't believe her.

Oh God. Rachel looked away. What if Meline was right? What if that engine blowing had been her fault and what if it'd happened on a turn and her brother had run into the wall? What if it'd caused Justin to stall completely and someone else had run into him?

Hugo seemed to be digesting all the information before coming to any conclusions, but he was skeptical. There was no doubt about it. Justin appeared plain angry, protecting her against all reason.

This was it. She couldn't do this anymore. She didn't want to cause anyone any more trouble, but she couldn't work for Meline one more minute. She had to make a stand. On her own two feet. Enough was enough.

Rachel stood. "I quit. As of right now, I don't work for Fulcrum Racing any longer."

"Wait a minute!" Justin jumped up.

"Figures." Meline shook his head.

"Don't do this, Rachel, honey," Hugo said.

Rachel walked out the door, feeling as if the world had fallen out from under her, and in a way it had. Fulcrum, NASCAR, engines, Hugo, Justin, this team, were all she lived and breathed.

Payton. No. The fact that he'd been purposefully keeping his distance these past few weeks stung. For her, for him, she shouldn't call him.

Charging outside to her truck, she dialed Kim's cell phone and got her voice-mail service.

Payton. He was still her friend. Her best friend. She needed him. Now more than ever.

CHAPTER TWENTY-THREE

IN THE MIDDLE of the weekly staff meeting, Payton's cell phone vibrated. He ignored it. It vibrated again, and again. Drawing it out of the case clipped to his waist, he found Rachel's home number illuminating the tiny screen. What was she doing at home? Something was wrong.

Jay watched Payton as if he expected some big break in the sports world. Payton mouthed, "I have to go." Jay nodded, and Payton rushed out of the conference room. He'd missed her call, and she hadn't left a message. When he dialed back, he got a busy signal. She had to be calling someone else.

Payton ran from his office building, climbed into his car and headed for the freeway. During the half-hour drive to Rachel's house, her home phone stayed busy, and she wasn't answering her cell. Possible scenarios raced through his mind. Could it be that Kim was back in the hospital? But then Rachel would've headed directly to Charlotte. Any kind of accident involving injuries and she wouldn't be at home. Meline. He would've put money on it.

He pulled into her driveway, noted her pickup parked outside the garage and ran toward the house. Holding a phone to her ear, she opened the front door before he had the chance to ring the bell. Her eyes were swollen and red and her face was blotchy. Obviously, she'd been crying. He resisted the urge to immediately draw her into his arms.

"Kim, I gotta go," she said into the phone. Pause. "Yeah, I'll be all right. Payton's here. Bye."

She set the phone down on top of a bookcase. The moment she glanced at him, her face filled with emotion, tears welled in her eyes, and she drew in a shaky breath.

Without saying a word, he stepped toward her. She fell into his open arms and buried her face in his chest. For several minutes, he held her while she sobbed. This had to be something big for Rachel to break down like this, and it wasn't about Kim. After a while he drew away and brushed the dampness from her cheeks. "What happened?"

"I…quit…my…job." The barely discernible words came out between shaky gulps of air.

"You quit Fulcrum?" he asked, not sure he'd heard correctly.

She nodded, a new wave of tears pouring down her face. Turning away, she headed into the kitchen.

Unbelievable. Quit the team. He followed her and waited while she blew her nose. "Why?"

She explained about disassembling the engine, finding the problem valve and relaying her suspicions about the exhaust system to the team during their conference to discuss Chicago's race results.

"So Meline, of course, tried to make a fool of you."

She nodded.

He'd like to get his hands on that piece of work. "Hugo didn't believe you?"

"I don't blame him. The exhaust system's a long shot and my theory is barely supported by our wind-tunnel tests."

"Then why did you quit?"

"I can't stand working for Meline one more minute. He's blaming me for the engine blowing on Sunday."

"Sweetheart, you know that's not true. You're the best engineer Fulcrum has on staff, and you're smarter than half the crew chiefs out there."

That caused a weak smile. "You don't know that."

"Yes, I do. Number one in your college class. I know how your mind works. And I've seen firsthand how hard you work for Fulcrum. For your uncle and brother. They need you. The way to stand up to Meline isn't by quitting. It's by going back. Fix that damned exhaust system. Fight Meline by proving him wrong. You know you can do it."

She rested her cheek against his chest, and the doorbell rang.

"Probably your uncle or your brother. Or both." He chuckled.

She opened the door and found Hugo and Justin standing on her front porch. Her uncle looked mad enough to spit tacks. "What the hell was that all about?" He charged into the living room. "Dammit, Rachel, you can't quit Fulcrum."

"I can and I did."

Rachel glanced back at Payton, and he grinned. *There's my Rachel.* Quitting might not be the right answer, but at least she was standing up to Hugo.

Hugo beaded in on Payton. "Did you put her up to this? Are you the one who talked her into quitting?"

Payton raised his hands in surrender and refused to say one word. Rachel could fight her own battles.

"He didn't have anything to do with this," she said. "Other than in helping me learn to stand up for myself."

"Quitting isn't the same as standing up for yourself,"

Hugo said, pacing back and forth. "Quitting is quitting. Giving up."

Rachel's face fell. Payton rubbed her back, but he kept quiet. She straightened her shoulders, brushed her cheeks dry and took a deep breath. "What did you expect me to do, Hugo? For months you've been staying out of the entire thing. It felt as if you were taking Meline's side."

"I knew he wouldn't come up with the fix." Hugo shook his head. "I was waiting for you to do it. All on your own. You ever want to be a crew chief, you gotta learn how to stand against the tide, Rachel. I know you got it in you." He walked toward the windows and stood gazing out at the lake.

Justin sighed. "He fired Meline right after you left."

Whoa! Even Payton knew that was a bold step, firing an engine builder midseason.

She didn't say anything, but surprise clearly registered in her gaze as she spun toward Justin looking for confirmation.

"You walked out the door," her brother went on, "and he fired him on the spot. Even before he asked Wade if he thought you could be right about the exhaust system."

Rachel turned toward her uncle. "I'm sorry. That it came to this."

"I'm the one who's sorry. I was pushing you to stand on your own two feet and you did. Meline wasn't listening." He turned toward her. "We need a new engine builder, Rachel. Will you do it? And, for now, be our specialist at the track, too. I know it's a lot of work, but I know you can handle it."

"You want me to be engine builder?"

"We need you."

"I need you," Justin said. "It's the only way I've got a shot at the championship."

Rachel looked to Payton.

He smiled and shrugged. "It's what you want."

"I'll think about."

There's my Rachel.

Hugo crossed his arms over his chest. "You're going to think about it?"

Rachel straightened. "You giving me leeway to make my changes? Starting with the exhaust manifold?"

"Depends on what they are."

"No, Hugo. That'd be jumping from the frying pan into the fire. Either you trust my judgment or you don't. And it seems to me that you don't."

"It's not that I don't trust you—"

"I want the same level of autonomy you gave Johnny."

"I'll work on it."

"Then I'll think about it."

"Rachel—"

Before Hugo could say anything more, Justin grasped his uncle by the arm and hauled him toward the door. "She said she'd think about it. That's good enough for me," he said with a wink and a lopsided grin at Rachel.

After they'd left, Rachel turned to Payton. "I don't know what to do."

"Of course you know."

"I'm not sure." She shook her head. "After I quit and walked out of that conference room, I realized there was a piece of me that felt incredibly relieved."

"Why? You love NASCAR. Your job."

"I do, I did. But my job, my schedule, is also the biggest thing…keeping you and me apart."

"It's not that simple."

"Yeah, it is. If I'm not dealing with NASCAR's hectic schedule, then if—when—you get your network show out in L.A. it'd be easier for us to still see each other. I could move out to L.A." She realized what she'd said and back-tracked. "I didn't mean…if—"

"Oh, Rachel. I'd take you with me everywhere, any-where I go." The clouds seemed to clear. This would solve everything. She could quit Fulcrum, leave NASCAR, work for some normal company. She'd have a life outside NASCAR, and they'd get a chance at making their rela-tionship work.

What about crew chief? What about her dream?

He shook his head. "I'd love to have you come with me, but your decision shouldn't be based on what I do." His way wasn't necessarily the right way for everyone. He laughed. "I can't believe I'm saying this, but sweet-heart, I was wrong."

He spread his arms wide and looked around her house. "What you've got here is a good thing. You belong in NASCAR. With Hugo and Justin at Fulcrum. You belong in this house. In this town. With these people." He brushed his fingertips over her cheek. "This is your life, Rachel. I couldn't live with taking you away from all this. It's where you belong."

A fresh batch of tears streamed down her cheeks.

"Engine builder gets you one step closer to being one helluva crew chief. If you don't take that promotion, you'll regret it for the rest of your life."

She knew he was right. He could see it in her eyes.

"Take the engine builder job. We'll still be able to see each other."

"Do you think?"

No. He didn't think. He knew. With the kind of commitment her job required and the kind of traveling out of the country his fantasy job would require, once he headed to L.A., they'd rarely ever see each other. Still, he couldn't get in the way of her decision, her dream.

"We'll find a way to make it work," he lied. "Go back to Fulcrum. Fix that exhaust system. Do what you can to help Justin win the championship. You can make a difference. I know you can."

Dammit all to hell. He was really going to miss her.

CHAPTER TWENTY-FOUR

"WHAT'S UP, DONNA?" Payton tapped his fingertips on his desktop.

"The NSN execs saw your special on the Murphys." His agent's voice sounded loud over the phone. Too loud. Too excited. "They couldn't believe the ten-percent increase in ratings. People love you."

His stomach flipped. This was what he'd been waiting for all these months.

"Are you sitting down?"

What a ridiculous question. He felt absolutely no patience this morning.

"You've got a contract offer from NSN."

He should be ecstatic, breaking out the champagne. Instead, he felt nothing, a surreal sense of nothing. "Already? I thought there'd be some negotiations before they actually made an offer."

"They really want you and they wanted to show you how serious they are. We'll consider their offer, and then we need to actually meet for further negotiations."

"How are the terms?"

"We've got a few things to nail down, but pretty good for a first shot."

"I want to do some NASCAR specials." That way he'd be sure to see Rachel a few times a year, at least.

A brief silence hung on the line. "I'm sure they'd be willing to talk about that."

"Are they giving me production control?"

"With some minor restrictions. This is it, Payton. This is it." She paused. "The only time for the next two weeks that they can get all their people together is Saturday night for dinner. Can you do that?"

He thought about his calendar. The race schedule. Rachel would be in Indianapolis on Sunday. He didn't want to miss the first race with her engine. "No. I'll be at the race in Indianapolis."

"Are you serious?"

What could he say? "I don't want to miss the race."

"Payton, this is what you've been working toward for months. The network has stepped out on a limb to make you feel wanted. If you don't make it out here on Saturday, they'll know where you stand, and you don't want to begin a new relationship on bad footing. You'll need their cooperation for every one of your projects. Do you want to do this, or not?"

IT WAS LATE, close to midnight, by the time Rachel left Fulcrum headquarters. If it killed her, she was going to get this new car, complete with an entirely new engine, ready for Sunday's race in Indianapolis.

Most of Mooresville was asleep, so there was no traffic to deal with on her way through town. By the time she reached her private drive, she'd relaxed, if only a little. Without streetlights, the woods seemed eerily deserted. When her headlights reflected off a car in her driveway, Rachel's heart skipped a beat.

Payton's car. She smiled and ran into her house. "Payton?"

"Out here." He was on her deck, sitting in a chair and facing the water. When she opened the screen, he glanced back. "Hope you don't mind. I…didn't want to be alone." There was a seriousness about him she'd never before seen or felt.

"What's the matter?"

For a moment, he didn't speak. She couldn't help but feel as if he were absorbing her, making her a part of him. "I got a contract offer today. From NSN."

She grabbed his hand and grinned. "That's wonderful. It's what you've wanted."

"I'm going out there this weekend to work through the details. I won't be able to make it to the race at Indianapolis."

She'd hoped he'd come, if not to the pits, at least to the track. Knowing he was around somewhere, anywhere, would've calmed her. "It's okay. We'll tape it."

"This is your big race. I wanted to be there."

"Payton. It's okay."

"It should be, but it's not." He stood and went to the deck rail. "I don't know what's happening to me."

"NASCAR fever. Hits the best of us."

"It's not NASCAR." He turned around. His eyelids grew heavy, as if he were hiding some emotion. "It's you."

She walked toward him and he opened his arms. Stepping between his legs, she rested her head on his chest and wrapped her arms around his waist. His heart was racing.

It made her think of her skipping stone and how rubbing it inexplicably calmed her. "I have something I want to give you. Be right back." Rachel ran upstairs. She was about to pick up her stone from the bedside table when she heard him behind her.

Payton stood in the doorway, as serious an expression on his face as she'd ever seen. He didn't look around this room, her bedroom, where he'd never been before and comment on the decor or the soothing tan-and-cream color scheme, or how nice it was that a cool nighttime breeze blew in off the lake and in through the open window. They could've been outside, or in a crowded bar or in the middle of Turn Three at Daytona. He kept his eyes only on her.

"I know we shouldn't," he whispered as if there were a houseful of people downstairs and they'd be found out any second. "I'm leaving. Gone already. It's selfish." He took a step toward her and stopped. "But I…" He swallowed, taking in the whole of her. "Don't want to leave without ever knowing…"

"How you feel," she finished for him.

His chest rose and fell. Fast. "Exactly." But he didn't move.

Rachel sensed he wouldn't go any further without her invitation. He wouldn't want to hurt her. The crazy thing? She was hurting already and he didn't even know it. She didn't want to add to that pain, a sense of the unknown. She didn't want to wonder, keep wondering, what it would feel like to make love with him, to feel him loving her the only way he could.

Stepping through the strip of moonlight cutting a bright swath across the middle of her bedroom, she reached for him, ran her hand under his T-shirt, felt his skin and wanted only to be closer. She unbuttoned her shirt, yanked it off and kissed him, moved her mouth over his, pressed her belly against his hard stomach.

His breathing turned ragged, but still, he didn't move. She pulled back. "Payton?"

"Are you sure, Rachel? Very, very sure?"

"Do I look sure?" She kissed his palm.

"You look positive."

"Feel sure?"

"Like heaven." He dipped his fingertips under the straps of her bra and deliberately moved them off her shoulders, lowered his head and kissed her. "And you taste like my dreams."

He picked her up, carried her across the room and lowered her onto the bed. "But tomorrow—"

"Shh." She pulled him down beside her. "I don't want to think about tomorrow."

Tonight, right now, in this moment, he was completely hers, body and soul, and she was his. All was right in the world.

THE SCENT OF FRESH COFFEE brewing nudged Payton awake, but the distant coo of a mourning dove threatened to lull him back to sleep. Lying on his side, his head buried in soft down, a light quilt tucked around him, he didn't want to move. His muscles felt liquid, his joints rubbery. His back didn't even hurt.

And then he remembered where he was. Rachel's bed. He remembered what they'd done together and he was on fire all over again.

Where was she, anyway? He wanted to feel her again, smell her, hold her close against him. With a smile on his face, he flipped over and glanced around.

He didn't have to look too far to find her. She was in this room, all right.

Pieces of her surrounded him like a warm sleeping bag on a frosty mountain morning. Lacy white curtains, feminine yet functional, draped around the windows and filtered the bright morning sun. Pictures hung on the wall, images of Justin, Kim and Hugo everywhere. NASCAR and Fulcrum Racing baseball caps hung on hooks by the door while the clothes she'd worn last night lay in a pool on the floor. A framed photo of her parents and her cell phone, with something black and greasy smudged along the side, sat on the bedside table, along with a flat, round rock—a skipping stone—and a wrench.

A wrench. His woman was a motorhead.

His woman.

He'd never believed it could happen, that he could feel this sense of possession, and along with it, this sense of completeness and belonging.

He imagined himself waking here, in Rachel's bed. Every morning. Day after day. Strangely enough, he felt no strangling sense of panic along with that mental image. No claustrophobic heaviness settled on his shoulders. No sweat bloomed on his brow. Only contentment settled in his gut at the possibility of having her body tucked in front of him, his lips against her neck. He was home. Settled. Settled in. Settled down.

Into Rachel's house. Rachel's life.

Settling? Settling for what?

He sat up and swung his feet onto the floor. He bent his head into his hands. This was Rachel's life. Not his.

What he wanted, his dream job, L.A., didn't fit in Rachel's life. And if he gave it all up? What about six months, two years or five years from now when he'd want a change? What then? Rachel wouldn't move. She might say she would for his sake, but she wouldn't be happy. Her feet were so firmly planted in this life it was hard to imagine uprooting and replanting her anywhere. Maybe for NASCAR, or her family, but certainly not for him. He couldn't ask her to do that for him.

He might be able to delay this current job offer, but eventually he'd be riding out of Dodge alone. So what was the point? Why go through all that pain? Why kid himself, or her? They had no future, and the longer he stayed with her, the more it was going to hurt. Bite the bullet. Now. Today.

For her sake, if not his own.

"Payton?" He'd miss hearing her say his name, soft and laced with a hint of North Carolina sweetness. He'd miss hearing her voice. "You all right?" She set two cups of coffee onto the bedside table and kneeled in front of him. Her cool hands wrapped around his and drew them away his face. "What's the matter?"

He gazed into her eyes. Sleepy eyes. Bed-head hair. He'd never seen a more beautiful sight in his life. He'd carry this moment, the way she looked, inside him for the rest of his life. It would have to do. Standing, he picked his jeans up off the floor and yanked them onto his legs. "Last night was a mistake."

RACHEL WENT MOTIONLESS. She watched him moving, tried to comprehend what was happening. At first, she didn't think she'd heard him correctly, and then his words sank in. Hard. The air left her chest in a whoosh. She felt as if she'd been punched in the gut.

"Last night wasn't fair to you," he said.

As if hearing him regret making love with her once wasn't enough, she had to hear it twice. Dumbfounded, she stood, remained still. This couldn't be happening. Her thoughts scattered. She couldn't form the right words, couldn't find her voice.

"You know we don't belong together. I shouldn't have let this happen."

He shouldn't have let this happen. He?

He pulled his shirt on over his head and Rachel's thoughts immediately flew to what it had felt like to take that shirt off of him, to kiss a trail up his chest. Last night hadn't been a mistake at all. Last night had felt, at least for Rachel, like the most right thing she'd ever done.

"I'll get out of your hair." He moved toward the door. "We can both move on."

There'd be no moving on for Rachel. Payton would be *moving on* alone. She'd already fallen in love with him.

"I guess it's a good thing I'll be moving to L.A." He double-timed it down the stairs. Somehow she managed to put one foot in front of the other and follow him into the hall. She stopped at the top of the steps and watched him put his hand on the knob, his head bent. "I'm sorry, Rachel." And without turning back, he left. He closed the door and he left.

Rachel swallowed. The most important thing in the world to her had just walked out the door, and she hadn't said a single word. Not one single damned word.

That was it! She was sick of standing there and taking it, taking anything from anybody. No more. She didn't care if everything that came out of her mouth made no sense whatsoever, it was coming out.

"Sorry, my ass." She ran back to her nightstand, snatched up her stone and shot outside.

He opened his car door.

"Payton Reese!" she yelled. "You stop right there." He was upset, all right, but she was downright angry. "Last night was absolutely not a mistake, and it hurts like hell that you'd suggest it." She pointed, shook her index finger at him. "And don't you dare tell me to move on."

"Rachel, don't do th—"

"*Don't* tell me what to do! I listened to you. Now you listen to me."

He clenched his jaw, set his mouth in a thin, straight line. In the past, encountering that rock-hard demeanor on anyone would've been enough to send her running for cover. Not today. Not with this man.

"You want to go to L.A.? Fine. Go. I would never want to hold you back from anything. I want you to make your dreams come true. Every single one of them. I want you to be happy. But breaking it off with me? Because you're moving? Well, that's…that's plain old…stupid. Stupid." She nodded.

"Stupid?" He shook his head. "You'll be traveling all over the States to races. I'll be traveling all over the world, gone for months at a time. Our schedules will be crazy. When are we supposed to see each other?"

"How should I know?" She stalked around the car and jabbed him in the chest. "But you breaking it off with me without giving us a shot says one thing and one thing only. You're running away."

He straightened his shoulders. "I've never run away from anything in my life."

"There's a first time for everything."

He shook his head. "You don't know what you're talking about."

"You love me, and you're scared."

At that, his eyes faltered.

"Say it. Say you don't love me."

He shoulders quickly rose and fell. "I don't love you."

"Liar."

"I don't love you!" he yelled.

"Big fat liar!"

"Rachel—"

"Don't you Rachel me." The anger quickly fizzled and panic set in. She was losing the most important battle of her life. Tears streamed down her face and she didn't care. "Payton, don't do this."

He tucked her hair behind her ear. "Goodbye."

"Wait." She tucked her stone in his hand. "Keep this."

He clenched it tight and drove away.

CHAPTER TWENTY-FIVE

RACHEL, AND, FOR THAT MATTER, most of the No. 448's Fulcrum team, put in several fourteen-plus-hour days in the garages in Mooresville, working on not only a new engine, but an entirely new car for the race in Indianapolis. Work, eat, sleep. Work, eat, sleep, barely. Work, eat, sleep, some more.

Rachel figured the less she thought of Payton the better. She had no clue where he was, no clue what he was doing. For the first time in her life, the ground under her feet seemed spongy and weak. Even when Kim had been in the emergency room at the hospital Rachel had still known who she was, where she was going and why. Focusing on the No. 448 car was now all she had, and she planned on making the best of it.

They finished with the new engine late Wednesday night. "Let's get her up on the dyno," she said.

They'd run the engine on a dynamometer machine for four or more hours at 9,000 RPMs to test its output. In the morning, they'd pore over computer printouts detailing the engine's performance and examine the overall engine and, in particular, the spark plugs. If there was still work to be done, they wouldn't have much time to make further adjustments before the haulers took the cars and drove through the night to get to Indiana.

Time was not on Rachel's side.

After getting the engine running on the dyno, the rest of the team went home and Rachel went back to her office to handle e-mails, phone messages and any number of other tasks she'd been avoiding the past few days. A few hours later, exhaustion and the total quiet of Fulcrum headquarters caught up with her. She fell asleep at her desk.

The next morning, Loren's voice startled her awake. "Rachel? You never went home?" As their tire specialist, he hadn't had much more than moral support to offer throughout the week, but he had been there all the same.

She shook her head. "Today's it. We don't get this engine figured out, we won't be ready for Sunday."

"How'd it do on the dyno?" Fred asked. As an all-around general mechanic, he'd been her right-hand man through all of this.

"Let's go find out."

It was early, so most of the staff hadn't yet made it in to work. Fulcrum's hallways were deserted. Hugo found them in main assembly. Immediately, she noticed he was getting antsy. "How'd we do?"

Rachel hoisted the engine off the dyno machine, unscrewed two spark plugs and examined them with a magnifying glass. "She's running better than any of Johnny's, but something's still not right."

"Still gumming up?" Loren asked.

She nodded.

"Why?" Fred asked.

"Not sure. If I had time on a chassis simulator, I could have all this figured out before practice runs on Friday."

"I've already run it by Dixon," Hugo said. "He won't okay the expense."

"There's a big surprise."

Hugo flipped through the computer printouts. "This engine is acceptable, Rachel. I don't want you making any more changes on the angles on that exhaust manifold."

"Why not?"

"It's too risky, and we don't have the time to mess around."

Reworking the manifold for the exhaust meant all eight pipes for all eight cylinders had to be exactly the same length, exactly the same diameter with exactly the same bends, otherwise they'd get back pressure on the exhaust and Justin wouldn't get the full power out of the engine.

"Hugo—"

"I don't want to hear it. Look through the details on these printouts. Unless you find some glaring problem, this engine's good to go." He turned around and headed toward his office.

Rachel waited until her uncle was well out of earshot before turning to Loren and Fred. Perfectionist or not, she couldn't do this alone. "I need your help."

"Doing what?" Fred asked.

"Changing those angles some more."

"Rachel, you sure?" Loren said. "You change this engine and Hugo'll hit the roof."

"I'm not suggesting we change that engine."

"You want another one, right?" Fred smiled.

She nodded. "We're bringing another backup motor with us to Indianapolis." It would take them and the rest of the team most of the day, but she was convinced she could— they all could—make a difference. "Don't tell Hugo."

THE PRACTICE RUNS for the No. 448 car on Friday afternoon at the track in Indianapolis went fairly well after some minor adjustments to the springs and track bar. Justin came in tenth in his qualifying run.

"Whatever you did to this engine, Rachel, is working pretty good," her brother said over his radio. "I'm feeling more power than I have most of the season."

"Bring her in, Justin," Hugo said.

Wade and Rachel examined the spark plugs, while Hugo and Justin stood by.

"The plugs are gumming up faster than they did on the dyno," she said.

"I see that," Wade said.

"What's the matter?" her uncle asked.

She held his gaze. "We can do better."

"Tenth is a respectable start," Wade said.

Respectable starts had so far this season led to disappointing finishes. "We need better than respectable to make sure we're in the Chase. If we don't win this race, we might as well quit now."

"What are you suggesting?" Hugo asked.

"The backup motor will run faster."

Hugo glared at her. "You built another backup? After I told you to let it go?"

"Yes, sir."

Her uncle rubbed his eyes. "We can't change engines now, not after qualifying."

"Yes, we can."

Wade shook his head. "But then we'll have to start at the back of the pack."

Rachel threw down her clipboard. "The only chance we've got at winning this race is with the backup motor."

"Then why didn't you put that one in to begin with?"

"We didn't have time to test it at the shop."

"How do you know it'll be better?"

"I know. I deepened the angle of the pipes in the exhaust manifold. I think it'll clear out faster."

"You *think*. You want us to put Justin in last position and run an untested engine." Hugo shook his head. "I'm getting too old for this."

"Well?" Rachel asked.

Hugo looked at Justin. "What do you think?"

"I trust Rachel's judgment," her brother said. "If she thinks it's best, then let's do it."

"Thanks, Justin."

He grinned at her. "You better be right, Rayray."

Hugo considered the two of them, as if he were coming to grips with something. "Go ahead. Put in the backup motor."

CHAPTER TWENTY-SIX

PAYTON SAT in the foyer of NSN's parent company, impatiently tapping his foot as he and Donna waited to be escorted to their contract negotiation meeting. The executives planned to cater dinner in their conference room, but the thought of food turned Payton's stomach. As if he could eat anything.

Several flat-panel television screens were mounted on a nearby wall, each of them tuned to a different station, irritating the hell out of him. He didn't give a hoot about the latest Hollywood gossip, the local news or some sappy movie. Especially not when Rachel was scheduled to be interviewed before the Indianapolis race.

Why in the world didn't they have NSN on one of the screens?

"What's got you so jumpy?" Donna asked.

"Nothing. I'm fine."

"Bull. You're so preoccupied, you're not even here."

Payton couldn't stand it. He snatched a remote and, hungry for Rachel's face, switched one of the monitors to the Saturday prerace commentary. If he couldn't see her, he'd at least get some information on Justin, the No. 448 car and the team. The regular commentators were talking through the drivers and their teams, one by one, covering anything new from last week's race.

Rachel, baby, you must be so nervous. He imagined her pacing, her normal prerace jitters revved a notch. This was showtime for her and her engine.

"You're really into this stuff, aren't you?" Donna said, making more of a statement than asking a question.

"Shh." He heard Fulcrum's name mentioned. They were talking about firing the previous engine builder and how team shake-ups generally don't bode well for driver performance.

"Changing the No. 448's engine after qualifying, though, that takes guts," the commentator said.

"Changed the engine?" That meant the No. 448 car would have to start in last position. If Justin placed well in this race, or won, Rachel would be a hero. If he lost, her career might be over.

Goose bumps broke out on his arms. Rachel was growing into her own beautiful skin, learning how to jump in with both feet. Like when they'd made love. Once she'd decided to open up to him, she'd given herself over so completely, so honestly, there hadn't been a wall, let alone a fence in sight. He'd thought the memories of making love with her would carry him through, help him move on. Instead they were going to haunt him forever.

"Hello, Payton. Donna." Richard Offerton, one of NSN's executive producers, arrived in the foyer.

The announcers were already discussing another driver, so Payton tore his gaze away from the TV. "Hello, Richard."

The producer directed them down the hall and proceeded with small talk. Payton shoved his hands in the pockets of his dress pants and found Rachel's flat stone. He rubbed it between his fingers and felt better, calmer.

He noticed the contemporary artwork, clearly on the expensive end, decorating the softly lit foyer and hallways. The decor was tastefully done in peach and pale green and several more flat-panel television screens were strategically mounted on the walls, such that NSN's stations were visible from anywhere in the office. State-of-the-art computers sat on each employee's desk and the atmosphere seemed upbeat and comfortable.

Early-evening sunlight streamed into the meeting room as they exchanged greetings with the network people handling the negotiations, an attorney and two staff members. Copies of contracts had been laid out on the table.

Payton sat down and absently paged through the stack of papers. Good thing Donna was here. He couldn't concentrate. His attention drifted to the TV. "Do you mind if we turn that to NSN's NASCAR program?"

"Not at all." Offerton powered up the TV, tuned in to the prerace program and muted the volume.

After several frustrating minutes, Payton grabbed the remote and put the volume low so he could hear.

"Payton?" Donna whispered.

"What?" He shrugged back at her. "You guys don't mind, right?"

"Oh, not at all." They shook their heads. "We're used to it."

The conversation turned to contract specifics and working out the details of Payton's first year of programming. He turned Rachel's stone between his fingers. The contract was fine, except for one thing. "I thought we agreed I'd be able to do some NASCAR specials."

"That was the original plan. But we recently closed a deal for exclusive NASCAR coverage. We'll have a dedicated team located in Charlotte. That means you'll be focusing entirely on other types of extreme sports."

"Does that mean you're hiring someone else to cover NASCAR?" The stone turned and turned.

Offerton nodded. "We're scouting talent as we speak."

"So I don't get to cover NASCAR at all?" Payton let that sink in. His first year of programming necessitated him traveling to South America, Alaska, Nepal and Africa covering some of the most elite alpinists alive today. It was exactly what he'd dreamed. But no NASCAR. No race tracks.

No Rachel.

In the silence of the conference room, the low volume of the TV echoed off the walls. "We were supposed to have Rachel Murphy, Justin Murphy's sister, here today," the commentator said, "to give us an overview of a stock-car engine."

He glanced at the TV, hoping to see her face. Why had she given him this stone, anyway? So flat, perfect for skipping.

"Engines 101, they called it," the commentator went on. "But Rachel's a no-show. Anyone else want to give it a shot?"

Surprise, surprise. He smiled inside.

"Listen," Offerton said, standing. "We'll let you two talk this over, Donna. Let us know when you've decided what you're going to do."

Payton gripped the stone between his thumb and forefinger, and felt how ideal it was for skipping, so ideal you'd never want to skip it. You'd never want to let it go.

Because you knew you'd never find a more perfect skipping stone in all your life.

Richard Offerton and his crew filed out of the room, and Donna turned to him, furious. "What is this all about—"

"No." Payton knew. He could never let Rachel go.

Her brow furrowed. "What do you mean, *no?*"

"I mean, no, I don't want the offer. No, I'm not interested. No, I'm not signing."

"Payton, this is exactly what you wanted."

Literally, Payton had climbed every mountain he'd ever wanted to climb. He'd made his record-breaking ascent of K2 and charted a new route on Cerro Torre. A strange sense of contentment seeped under his skin. He suddenly felt no need to make a name for himself with some wild extreme sports show.

"Used to want, Donna. Things change. I've changed." He only hoped Rachel's feelings hadn't.

TEN LAPS TO GO here in Indianapolis, one of NASCAR's most exciting races of the season. Dean Grosso's been leading most of the race, but the surprise of the day is Justin Murphy moving from last place into second. He's been keeping the No. 414 car on his toes.

I'll tell ya, Justin needed today. They've had one problem after another with the No. 448's engines but, today, it looks as if they may have figured things out.

Rumor is Fulcrum Racing had a crew change. What do you hear about that?

That's no rumor. They outright fired their last engine builder. Justin's sister, Rachel Murphy, is now responsible for this new car setup.

No kidding.

Rachel's got a lot of experience. My guess is she'll be in charge of her own team someday. I wouldn't put it past her to be NASCAR's first woman crew chief.

Three to go—

The No. 448 car's making a move.

Not yet. The No. 414 car won't let him by.

Two to go and Murphy's taking Dean Grosso on the outside.

Look at the speed! He's been holding back.

That is one fast car.

He did it! Justin Murphy wins!

Oh, this is a big one for Fulcrum Racing. For Justin and his sister, Rachel.

It sure is.

Puts them back into Cup contention.

The Murphys are back in the Chase.

"Woohoo!" The pit crew went wild. Jumping. Hugging. Screaming. "We did it!"

"Way to go, Rachel!" She felt big, strong arms squeeze around her, felt her feet leave the pavement. "*You* did this, honey." Hugo smiled into her eyes. "You put your neck out, made a risky-as-hell call. And you were right. Be proud. I sure am." He set her down and moved on to the rest of the team.

Fred and Loren appeared next to Rachel, beaming. "You guys did good," she said, hugging each of them in turn. She let herself get jostled around and slapped on the back.

A momentary thrill rushed through her. She was happy for Justin, for Hugo and the team. They'd all worked so hard for this, not only this past week, but for months before that, before the beginning of the season. None of this would've happened without all their hard work this last week. She felt more a part of a team than ever before.

She only wished she could share in everyone else's enthusiasm. Instead, none of it mattered anymore. Payton wasn't here. He'd be back in Charlotte to pack his things, but for all intents and purposes, the man was gone. When it got right down to it, he'd never really been here to begin with. His heart had been in California the whole time.

The team was heading for Victory Lane. Rachel pasted a smile on her face and fell into step with the rest of her team. She couldn't let her own personal problems ruin this day for anyone else.

Maybe she shouldn't have gotten mad at Payton. Maybe she should've bitten her tongue. Instead, she'd sent him off angry, determined to get away from her.

They surrounded the No. 448 car. Justin threw out his helmet and climbed out. "Oooooeeee!" he yelled. "It's about damned time!"

Several corks popped and champagne rained down on the crowd. Someone poured a bubbling stream over Justin. He dumped some more over Rachel. She laughed. Wiped the sticky, cold liquid off her cheeks. Without warning, her throat closed and tears bubbled to the surface. She wanted to share this with Payton. He'd become such a NASCAR nut. Didn't he want to share it with her?

A reporter stuck a mike in front of Justin's face. "Feeling good?"

"Real good!" He hooted.

"You've been having a tough season so far. A lot of problems with your engines. How'd you move up from last place to win this race?"

"Ask my big sister. She built this engine." Justin jerked

Rachel against him and squeezed her around the shoulders. "*She* won this race! Ask her how it feels."

With that the reporter turned to her and put the mike in her face. "Rachel? You replaced Johnny Meline?"

She stared at the mike and froze.

"You built this engine?"

It was her engine. Yes. "Yes, sir."

"What did you change?"

She could do this. Nothing could possibly be as hard as losing Payton. "The exhaust manifold needed some work. We're still working out some kinks with the new car design."

"Congratulations, Rachel."

"Thank you."

The reporter moved to Hugo. "Is the NASCAR Sprint Cup Series championship looking closer?"

"You got that right—"

"Rachel!" Someone yelled her name from the crowd. She barely heard the voice. "Rachel!" That time it was louder, clearer.

"Payton?" Frantic, she glanced past the bodies swarming around her. "Where are you?"

"Over here." He pushed through the crowd.

"Oh, God, Payton." Tears streamed down her face. "When did you get here?"

"I caught the first flight out of L.A. this morning. Arrived in time for the last hour of the race."

"You saw the finish?"

"I couldn't miss it. Weird, huh?"

"Hey, Payton!" Justin yelled.

"You did it, man," Payton yelled back. "Congratulations!"

"No." Justin pointed at Rachel. "She did it."

Payton looked down into her face, cupped her cheeks. Bodies pushed against them. Champagne and confetti streamed through the air. The sounds of yelling surrounded them. All of it, everything, disappeared when she gazed into his eyes.

"I can't believe you came back," she said.

"I can't believe I ever left. And I don't ever want to leave you again," he said. "Marry me?"

Her tears fell harder and she nodded. "I think I'm ready to leave all this. It doesn't mean anything without you."

"I don't want you to leave NASCAR. I would never ask that."

"Then what are you saying?"

"I'm not moving to California."

"Oh, no, you don't." She shook her head and pulled him away from the crowd. She found a relatively quiet spot out of the mayhem and paced in front of him. "Don't you dare do this because of me. I couldn't live with you not making your dreams come true."

"Dreams can change."

Angry, she pushed against his chest. "You won't be happy if you don't take that job."

"You're wrong. I was wrong. I won't be happy if I do." He looked around and laughed. "The whole time I was in California, every waking minute, all I could think about was being back here. With you. These people. This thrill. This whole crazy mess. Your house. Lake Norman. North Carolina. It's all become part of my life. I'm hooked on NASCAR, Rachel. Hooked on you." He rested his forehead against hers. "You've become my life. Without you, not a thing makes sense anymore."

"That's how I felt without you." She squeezed him with everything in her, rested her head on his chest. "What are you going to do?" His heartbeat was even, solid, strong.

"Turns out NSN needed a new NASCAR man," he said. "As of today, I'm it. I'll still be doing a network show, but it'll be all about NASCAR. Here's the best part. Stationed in Charlotte. I'll be traveling to the tracks with you." He didn't have to stop moving. He'd be moving with Rachel.

"You're sure?"

"I love you, Rachel. I've never been more sure of anything in my life." He stepped back from her, placed his hands on either side of her face. "Will you settle for me? For the rest of your life."

"Settle? For you?" She nodded. "I can do that. You sure you can *settle* for me?"

"Settle down. Settle in." Yeah, he was settling, all right, and he couldn't be happier about it. He'd found a lover and a best friend all in one wonderful package. What more could any man want? "It took me a while, but I finally figured it out." He slipped her skipping stone into the palm of her hand and squeezed his own fingers around hers. "I'm not settling for anything less than perfection."

* * * * *

For more thrill-a-minute romances set against the exciting backdrop of the NASCAR world, don't miss

OUT OF LINE by Michele Dunaway,
available in June

For a sneak peek, just turn the page!

"WERE YOU AND YOUR FATHER close?" Lucy asked.

Sawyer blinked once. "I don't know. Now that the blinders are off, it's like dawn chased away the darkness, but the picture I can see isn't pretty. My father used my mother for her connections early in her marriage and then, since divorce isn't cheap and would have ruined his social status, simply replaced her with the younger, prettier model on the side. That's the only explanation I can come up with."

"I'm sorry," Lucy said.

His tone sharpened. "I don't want your pity. Heck, I'm telling you things I shouldn't be. You'll never want to go out with me again. You'll think I'm off my rocker."

Lucy shook her head and tightened her grip on Sawyer's hands. "Never. In fact, I'm glad you're opening up to me. It lets me know who you really are. I don't like secrets. I've seen the harm they do to relationships."

"Yeah. Just look at my family."

"We have to be so strong and tough, but everyone has vulnerabilities. It's the man who can admit his weaknesses who impresses me, not Mr. Invincible who I know is only putting on a brave front."

"I don't want you in the role of a therapist," Sawyer said. "I'd like to date you, not unload on you."

She could appreciate his concern. That would create an unhealthy relationship. "Don't worry. That's not going to happen. My listening when you have a problem is what friends do."

"I don't want to stop at friends," Sawyer said. "You're very special." He used his free hand to cover their joined hands, giving Lucy that warm and fuzzy feeling deep inside.

"Thanks." They stayed like that for a moment before reluctantly breaking contact so they could finish eating.

Lucy relaxed as lunch went on. One thing had become clear. Her connection with Sawyer went further than just a surface, physical link.

"You'll all get past this thing with your father," she encouraged.

He nodded. "I know. My sister and her husband had separated for a while, but they're back together. Bart and Will have new sponsors. I'm worried about my mother. I haven't seen her in a while and I don't have a free weekend until June. I've called, and when we talk I can tell all this has been very rough on her."

"I can't imagine what she's going through."

"Neither can I. Bart told me he's trying to hook her up with his financial manager. If my mom says yes, hopefully the guy will be able to do some good and help my mom out."

"I hope so," Lucy said, not offering advice. Instead she let Sawyer talk.

"It would have been so much simpler if my father had been killed. You know, died in a private plane crash or something. Does that sound horrible of me? If he'd died, the scandal wouldn't have been half as juicy. Instead he's a fugitive for white-collar crime, only my mother's true friends have stayed by her, our lives have made the tabloids, we've been publicly humiliated by Alyssa Ritchie and we'll have to endure more when she publishes that memoir. What was she thinking, breaking up my family?"

Lucy didn't have an answer to that. "Twenty years is a long time."

"I will never do that to my wife or my family," Sawyer declared forcefully. He reached out and grabbed her hands. His black eyes seemed like pools of liquid obsidian as he held her gaze. "Never."

She nodded, seeing the truth there in his eyes. Sawyer was a one-woman man. He'd never be anything but. "I believe you won't."

"Good." They sat perpendicular to each other, and Sawyer leaned over the corner of the table and brought his face closer to hers. He dropped the lightest of kisses onto her lips before easing back into his own space.

That feather touch shattered her. The promise in the kiss and in his eyes had been genuine. The kiss, while brief, shook her to the core with the sensations it evoked. Her toes had actually curled. Sure she'd dated, but she'd never experienced anything like this before.

He didn't apologize for the public display of affection, for the light touch that had branded her as his.

She was a little overwhelmed by the emotions she was experiencing. She'd like nothing more than to take Sawyer back to her apartment and rip his T-shirt and jeans off. Yet at the same time, he'd caught her up in the romance. He'd shared his deepest feelings and he'd treated her with respect. As an equal.

This was new ground. Unfamiliar, exciting territory. Could he be the right man? Only time would tell, but the possibilities suddenly seemed endless.

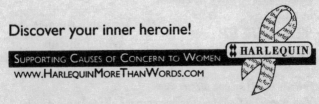

"Aviva gives the best bear hugs!"

—Jennifer Archer, author

*Jennifer wrote "Hannah's Hugs," inspired by Aviva Presser, founder of **Bears Without Borders**, a nonprofit organization dedicated to delivering the comfort and love of a teddy bear to severely ill and orphaned children worldwide.*

Look for "*Hannah's Hugs*" in
More Than Words, Vol. 4,
available in April 2008 at eHarlequin.com
or wherever books are sold.

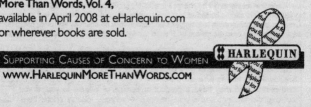

SUPPORTING CAUSES OF CONCERN TO WOMEN ⧸⧸ HARLEQUIN
WWW.HARLEQUINMORETHANWORDS.COM

REQUEST YOUR FREE BOOKS!

2 FREE NOVELS PLUS 2 FREE GIFTS!

SPECIAL EDITION®

Life, Love and Family!

YES! Please send me 2 FREE Silhouette Special Edition® novels and my 2 FREE gifts (gifts are worth about $10). After receiving them, if I don't wish to receive any more books, I can return the shipping statement marked "cancel." If I don't cancel, I will receive 6 brand-new novels every month and be billed just $4.24 per book in the U.S. or $4.99 per book in Canada, plus 25¢ shipping and handling per book and applicable taxes, if any*. That's a savings of at least 15% off the cover price! I understand that accepting the 2 free books and gifts places me under no obligation to buy anything. I can always return a shipment and cancel at any time. Even if I never buy another book from Silhouette, the two free books and gifts are mine to keep forever.

235 SDN EEYU   335 SDN EEY6

Name _____ (PLEASE PRINT)

Address _____ Apt. #

City _____ State/Prov. _____ Zip/Postal Code

Signature (if under 18, a parent or guardian must sign)

Mail to the **Silhouette Reader Service:**
IN U.S.A.: P.O. Box 1867, Buffalo, NY 14240-1867
IN CANADA: P.O. Box 609, Fort Erie, Ontario L2A 5X3

Not valid to current subscribers of Silhouette Special Edition books.

Want to try two free books from another line?
Call 1-800-873-8635 or visit www.morefreebooks.com.

* Terms and prices subject to change without notice. N.Y. residents add applicable sales tax. Canadian residents will be charged applicable provincial taxes and GST. Offer not valid in Quebec. This offer is limited to one order per household. All orders subject to approval. Credit or debit balances in a customer's account(s) may be offset by any other outstanding balance owed by or to the customer. Please allow 4 to 6 weeks for delivery. Offer available while quantities last.

Your Privacy: Silhouette is committed to protecting your privacy. Our Privacy Policy is available online at www.eHarlequin.com or upon request from the Reader Service. From time to time we make our lists of customers available to reputable third parties who may have a product or service of interest to you. If you would prefer we not share your name and address, please check here. ☐

SSE08R

Love Inspired
SUSPENSE
RIVETING INSPIRATIONAL ROMANCE

REUNION REVELATIONS

Secrets surface when old friends—
and foes—get together.

Look for these six riveting Reunion Revelations stories!

Hidden in the Wall
by VALERIE HANSEN
January 2008

Missing Persons
by SHIRLEE McCOY
February 2008

Don't Look Back
by MARGARET DALEY
March 2008

In His Sights
by CAROL STEWARD
April 2008

A Face in the Shadows
by LENORA WORTH
May 2008

Final Justice
by MARTA PERRY
June 2008

Available wherever books are sold.

Steeple
Hill®